The MIRROR

INTRODUCTION

Cats are often referred to as the jerks of the pet world—aloof and refusing to do what they're told. Yet those of us who love cats see them differently. To us, they're independent souls who don't take crap from anyone. They're the contradiction of the animal world—loving souls who will purr one minute as you caress them and then claw the hell out of your hand for daring to touch them. Yet we adore cats when they're cuddled on our laps while we read and drink our tea, or those times when they sit behind us, warming our necks and souls. There is something so special about that curled up bundle of purring fur that just soothes the soul and gives us moments of peace, warmth, and tranquility.

In literature and pop culture, cats are seen as adventurers, heroes, and even villains. Who can forget about Lucifer in Disney's *Cinderella* who tries to eat Cinderella's beloved mice? Or Scar in *The Lion King* who murders Mufasa? Cats can also be morally gray, tricksters like Cheshire in *Alice's Adventures in Wonderland* and *Through the Looking Glass*. If you want a fun version of Cheshire, check out *Lost in a Good Book* by Jasper Fforde. Then there's Cat in *Breakfast at Tiffany's*, Crookshanks from J.K. Rowling's Harry Potter franchise and Hobbes, the stuffed tiger that comes to life in a boy's imagination from *Calvin and Hobbes*.

It's generally assumed that cats can sense the unusual, and many of our authors took advantage of this idea such as Kari Shuey & Angela Perry in *Off Balance* and in Lara Yamada's *The Dreamwalker*.

Then there's the mirror aspect! Throughout time, we've wondered if mirrors might be gateways to other realms. They're seen as a bridge or an entrance to a magical place or a place that exists only in the mind. Mirrors are often viewed as a transition, that place between consciousness and unconsciousness when anything—any thought, any view, any idea—is possible.

We use mirrors to tell us the truth of our physical selves, yet acknowledge the view is reversed and thus not accurate. I don't think any of us disagree that mirrors have the ability to show us things we don't want to see about ourselves or others. Sometimes mirrors can force us into an awareness that can be troubling. Or maybe that awareness is freeing, allowing us to see the world differently or let things that don't really matter go.

And yet, mirrors can help us lie, as any stage magician will tell you. That wonderfully iconic ballroom scene at Disneyland's Haunted Mansion, where the ghosts are twirling throughout the room, is done with mirrors. Interior decorators also use mirrors to increase the light in a dark room or give the illusion of space in a tiny apartment.

And what about those times when you catch a glimmer of movement in a mirror and spin around to find nothing there? What about those moments when you wonder what might happen if you could reach your hand through a mirror and into... something else? Those moments of "what was that?" are explored in A.E. Santana's *Night Mews, Grandma Ruth's*

Legacy by Donna Marie West, and *Reflections of Hawthorne* by Donna Keeley.

Mirrors also give us the chance for transformation, as any beautician will tell you when they spin a client around to show off a new make-up or hair style. *Beloved Queen* by Dennis K. Crosby and *Panther Stares Back* by Evan Baughfman explore the concept of using mirrors to become more than one is.

In literature and pop culture, mirrors abound, from the Magic Mirror dooming a young princess in *Snow White*, to the mirror Alice steps through in *Through the Looking Glass*. *The Picture of Dorian Gray* uses a mirror to allow Dorian to always remain young. And then there's the dark side of mirrors explored in horror movies such as in *Poltergeist* and more recently in Jordan Peele's *Us* (admit it, you just shivered!).

And in this anthology, we decided to combine cats and mirrors by opening the call with this prompt:

> *The mirror that hung in her bedroom belonged to her grand-mother. She'd always been told there was something special about it and her cat seemed to think so too.*

We told our authors they didn't have to use it verbatim, though several did, but could use it as a jumping off point to inspire them. We left the genre open, and our wonderful authors delivered with a fun collection of fantasy, such as Miriya Greer's *This isn't an Illusion*, urban fantasy, such as S. Faxon's *The Whisper Ones*, sci-fi, such as Chris Bannor's *For Yours*, horror, such as K.R. Cervantez's *Grave Demise*, and contemporary stories with a slight supernatural bent such as *Marla* by Rick Powell. Some of these stories are laugh-out-loud funny, some will give you the heebie-jeebies when your cat stares off into a mirror, and others will need you to have the tissue box close by. We guarantee you won't look at mirrors or your cats the same way after reading this collection.

Finally, a huge thank you to everyone who submitted. We've greatly enjoyed working with each of you through the editing process and have loved seeing what you come up with when you get feedback such as, "this ending just doesn't quite work—can you tie it back more to the promise the introduction makes?" The success of this anthology wouldn't be possible without each of you, so thank you for putting your time and energy into not only writing these stories but providing us with the edits and helping us with the marketing. Thank you for sharing a piece of your time, your creativity, and your souls with us.

Sarah (S. Faxon) and I invite you to find your favorite reading spot, grab the beverage of your choice, and enjoy The Mirror!

Theresa Halvorsen

Beloved Queen
By Dennis K. Crosby

She saw the blow coming, but with a second guy pointing yet another gun at her, there wasn't much for Reggie to do other than brace and take the hit. The sting of the pistol connecting with her forehead was delayed, but when it arrived, it came with a few seconds of blurred vision. The butt of the gun was hard, and she was certain she felt a cut open across her forehead from the jagged metal. It was disorienting; then came the ringing in her ears.

This was not how she'd planned her day.

She'd come to Rogers Park to move the final item from her grandparent's home. Her grandfather had passed away just one month prior. He'd been Reggie's last surviving grandparent. They'd been close over the years, the later years. Growing up, Reggie had felt her grandfather was too busy for her. She'd thought the success he'd achieved came with a wall that kept the old man isolated. Isolated and unreachable. That wasn't the case, but it was Reggie's perception and at the time, and with a teenager's point of view, it was all that mattered. Later, with some age and a little wisdom, she would see the truth of things. And that truth allowed her to have a solid five years with him. Five years of laughter, of travel, of learning, and of love. She'd cherished that time, as grateful for those five years as she was during every moment with her grandmother before her grandmother had passed. Her grandparents were very special people, and they'd both left her something in their wills. They were well off, and for some reason, there'd been rumors of hidden treasures everywhere.

Hence the home invasion Reggie now experienced.

"Now, I'm gonna ask you one more time, dammit! Where'd the old man keep his money?" asked the lead gunman.

Reggie knew this guy from the neighborhood. Chris Stone, local bad guy, and all-around asshole. He'd never had an honest day's work in his life. If he didn't beg, borrow, or steal —mostly steal—he'd have nothing. People in the neighborhood feared him. He had a short fuse and was unpredictable. If he was displeased, there'd be hell to pay. Sweat rolled down his bald head. His chocolate skin looked clammy. He was tweaking.

Great!

"I'm telling you, there's no money in this house. Look at it! This place is empty!"

The house was nestled on the corner of a dead-end street, just meters away from Lake Michigan. It was a well-kept, two-story residence with a detached two-car garage. With a covered wraparound front porch, you could sit outside, in almost any weather and just enjoy the day. Reggie's grandfather had particularly loved sitting out there on rainy days. He'd smoke cigars, have a drink, play some music, and listen to the rainfall, and the crash of the waves on the lake. It was indeed a beautiful and comfortable home, one of many her grandparents owned. But it was empty now. Her grandparents had donated the furniture and artwork upon their deaths. There was only one item remaining, a gift to Reggie from her grandmother. The home now belonged to her, too—a gift from her grandfather.

Another smack across the head reminded Reggie that her answer was unacceptable.

"C'mon man, stall her out," said the second gunman.

Will was his name. He was from the neighborhood too, but Reggie had never known his last name. He was a quiet guy. More of a follower than a leader. He'd come from a good family. One of those southern Baptist families that went to church every Sunday for worship, every Tuesday for choir practice, and every Wednesday for bible study. Seems none of that stuck with Will, though. Still, Reggie sensed hesitance in him. Maybe, just maybe, the man had a conscience.

She could use that.

"What? Who do you think you're talkin' to?" asked Chris.

"Beatin' her ain't gonna get us what we came for," said Will.

"Well, askin' her nicely obviously ain't gonna get it, either. Stop bein' so damned soft!"

Reggie couldn't tell if they were playing good cop, bad cop, or truly at odds about the current methods being used. Either way, she figured she'd better chime in.

"Look, guys, I'm tellin' you, there's nothing here. No furniture, no art, no nothing. Everything was donated. The walls are bare. Look around. Not a wall safe to be found. The only thing left is a mirror."

"A mirror?" asked Chris.

"Yeah. A mirror."

Reggie thought back to the first time she'd heard about her grandmother's most prized possession. It was shortly before her grandparents had moved to Rogers Park. The day she'd gone searching for Jasper because it was time to go home.

Where was that damned cat, anyway?

He was old, well, older, but still active. *Very* active. Jasper liked to wander the house when they came through. She was certain he'd explored every corner in the place over the years and probably found spots long since forgotten.

At least he was safe.

"What's wrong, girl?"

Reggie crossed her arms and turned away from her grandmother.

"Oh no. We are not doing this today."

Regina felt her eight-year-old body being lifted, turned, and set back down. The view was no longer the rainy streets of Rogers Park. Now, the view was her grandmother, with a faint grin, and a raised eyebrow. Reggie knew what that look meant. It was a challenge, a demand, and compassion, somehow rolled into one expression. Her arms were still crossed, but Reggie felt her resolve breaking.

"Let's hear it."

"I..." began Reggie.

Now, she felt her arms being uncrossed and the comfort of her grandmother's hands holding hers. Her resolve was fully broken now. It wasn't that hard. Eight was a tough age to be. These days, she held out about fifteen seconds longer than she had at age seven. It wasn't that she was shy or embarrassed. Reggie just did not like to seem weak. The youngest of five children, and the only girl, she always felt in competition with her brothers. In her mind, sadness, and complaints were weaknesses.

And she would have none of it.

"What is it, baby girl?"

"I... hate my name," said Reggie with a heavy, venomous emphasis on the word hate.

"You hate your name? Sweet Jesus, child. Why?"

"Because it's a boy's name. And I'm not a boy."

"Oh honey, come here."

Reggie felt her grandmother pull her in for a hug. Safe in those loving arms, the tears began to fall. More weakness. In that moment, though, she didn't care. If she were being honest, she never cared about weakness when in the safety of her grandmother's arms.

"Are the kids making fun of you? Is that it?"

Reggie nodded her head swiftly; the way children do when in an embrace and crying impedes their ability to speak. She pushed her head against her grandmother even more to muffle the sound.

"Oh, sweetie. I'm sorry." The hug tightened.

The comfort increased.

"Tell me something. Do you know what your name means?"

Reggie shook her head.

"Come with me, honey, let's talk about this. And when we're done, you'll never hate your name again."

"Where we goin', Grandma?"

But her grandmother said nothing. It didn't matter. It wasn't as if Reggie would refuse to go. Maybe she'd finally get a chance to see the mirror everybody talked about. Well, more like, whispered about. The infamous mirror that hung in the bedroom. It belonged to her grandmother. She'd always been told there was something special about it, and her cat seemed to think so, too. She'd always brought Jasper with her on visits. In this old house, on the west side of Chicago, he'd always be missing. And when she'd call for him, he always seemed to be coming from the bedroom.

Maybe today, she'd learn why.

"You don't have to do this, you know? Talk to your boy, convince him to leave, and I won't press charges. The police will never know you'd been here. I promise," said Reggie.

She looked back slightly as she ascended the stairs with the second gunman, Will, hoping to appeal to his good nature. She was certain there was something inside him that was redeemable. But he said nothing, just continued on, occasionally pushing her in the back with his weapon to remind her he was armed.

As if she needed the reminder.

They got to the top of the stairs and turned right, walking down the hall to her grandfather's office. It had doubled as a sitting room when her grandma, Mary, was alive. That room was special. No, not the room; it was the item inside the room that was special. The mirror was the true treasure. The mirror needed protection.

Soon, the thieves would need protection, too.

Reggie walked hand-in-hand with her grandmother to the second floor. She loved the house her grandparents lived in. They'd only recently moved there from the west side of Chicago, where Reggie and her family still lived. She wished they'd live in this new place all year long, but the Midwest winters were too much for them to manage. Every year, right after Thanksgiving, Reggie's grandparents packed up, flew to San Diego, and for six months they'd live in an area called Encinitas. Reggie visited once. It was beautiful. They had an amazing view of the ocean in their three bedroom condo. Reggie wanted to live there one day. One day, she would leave this city and all the bullies. One day, she would be something different. One day, she would be *someone* different.

One day.

Reggie and her grandmother entered a room that served as a sitting room for her grandmother, and an office for her grandpa. He was a writer. A fairly famous one, apparently. People knew him well, and a few of his books had been made into movies and television shows. In fact, he was out of the house today to meet with his agent who'd flown in for a special meeting with a producer who wanted to make a movie about a book he hadn't even finished yet.

Reggie wanted to do that, too.

She loved making up stories. She loved creating worlds where anything was possible. Most often, in her worlds, she was strong, powerful, and no one dared make fun of her, or her name.

In the sitting room was the mirror. Reggie's eyes widened.

"Grandma, is that the mirror everyone talks about? I thought it was in your bedroom."

"It used to be, honey. But I decided to move it here. We made some adjustments to it, me, and your grandpa. We added some braces, so now it's free standing. See those braces in the middle? Those allow it to tilt in the middle. See?"

Reggie nodded.

The mirror was rectangular and framed in an intricate reddish-brown wood. The edges of the mirror were—what the adults called—beveled. Reggie heard the word once and thought it sounded fancy. It was old, from what Reggie was told, but still looked brand new. It looked like it was fresh from the package, or just made that day.

Reggie's grandmother moved to sit on the floor, then gestured for Reggie to join her. Reggie sat and rested her head against her grandmother's arm as they both stared at each other's reflection.

"Now," began her grandmother, "you tellin' me you really don't know what your name means?"

Reggie shrugged.

"I'm sure I've told you before."

"I forgot," said Reggie softly.

"That's okay, honey. I promise you, after today, you'll never forget again."

Reggie felt a cool breeze move through the room. Outside, the rain intensified. She heard a slow roll of thunder, and her heartbeat increased. It was not from fear but from euphoria. Reggie always felt better when it rained. Flashes of lightning and cracks of thunder energized her. Where most kids hated it, because it meant they had to stay inside, Reggie reveled in it, because in this moment, she felt like mother nature was speaking directly to her.

"So, your full name is Regina Marie Devereaux. Your middle name, Marie, is a form of my name."

"Mary?"

"That's right."

"So, I'm kind of named after you?" asked Reggie.

"Kind of, yeah. But *we* are both named after someone else. A woman in our family line's name was Marie."

"It was her first name?"

"Mm-hmm. And lots of the girls in her family line had the name Marie or Mary as their first or middle name. And that name means beloved."

"What does beloved mean?"

"It means that everybody, and I mean *everybody*, loves you."

Reggie felt her grandmother squeeze her tight as she said those words, and it forced a smile. She didn't want to, but she could not help it. And that... was okay.

"What about my first name?"

"Oh, now your first name, baby girl, is something extra special. The name Regina means queen."

"Like, Amidala from Star Wars?"

"Yes," began Mary, shaking through a giggle, "just like her. Only, not in a galaxy far, far away."

Reggie laughed out loud and continued to stare at their reflections in the mirror. She let the words roll in her mind and thought about them over and over.

Regina Marie.

Queen.

Beloved.

"Beloved Queen," whispered Regina.

Reggie felt another squeeze from her grandmother, and she smiled again. As she continued to stare at her reflection, she saw their images distort, then fade into a gray cloud. A new image formed, and this time, it was not her sitting on the floor with her grandmother. It was her, sitting on a throne, with hundreds of people kneeling. This new image of Reggie was older. Not quite an adult but definitely older. The image stared back at Reggie, smiled, and stood. The woman began to walk toward her, getting closer and closer.

"Grandma?"

"Yes, child?"

"What's happening?"

Her grandmother remained silent. The image of the older Reggie kept coming and eventually filled the entire mirror. Looking closer, Reggie realized it wasn't her, but a woman who looked a lot like her. The other woman's dark hair fell in curls against her light brown skin. She wasn't a queen, but she was regal, and revered... and loved. Reggie was afraid, but only a little. Curiosity filled her more than fear.

Even when the woman in the mirror reached out beyond the reflective surface.

In a matter of seconds, Reggie saw a non-corporeal image of the woman standing before her. It coalesced into vapor and flew directly at Reggie, entering her body. Reggie felt warmth in her chest, then her arms and legs, and finally her fingers and toes. She closed her eyes and let the sensation fill her. Several minutes passed until a crack of thunder forced her eyes open. Directly across from her, in the mirror, was the image of her sitting next to her grandmother.

Only Reggie's eyes were now gold.

When they got to the office, Reggie heard her cat just beyond the door. Likely staring into that mirror. She wondered what he saw in the reflection.

Will pushed Reggie through the door, causing her to stumble. The sudden noise startled Jasper, who jumped back from the mirror into a defensive posture, front paws spread, fangs bared, bearing down with his tail in the air. The orange tabby stared at Reggie, giving occasional looks to the gunman behind her. It was as if he was assessing the situation and trying to determine how best to help his mother.

Typical Jasper.

"What's the deal?" asked Will.

"What do you mean?"

"Why is this house completely empty of everything except for this mirror?"

"The mirror is the last to go. They left it to me, and it requires... special shipping."

"Special how?"

"You can't just box this up and mail it. It has to be packed just right and shipped with care."

"And just what is so special about it?"

Will walked closer to it. Reggie watched as he touched the wood frame and the glass. He was lost in thought as he stared at his reflection, but Reggie was pretty certain he saw nothing. At least, not the things she could see.

"Did you find it?"

Will jumped at the words of his partner, standing behind them. Reggie sized Will up again and wondered how someone so skittish got into the business of home invasions. He didn't seem the type. Everything about him still screamed compassion. He wasn't innocent. She was certain of that. He'd done things and justified them. That's likely what was happening now. At his core, he felt he was doing it *for* something.

Or someone?

"What the hell is this?" asked Chris.

"It's the only thing in here. There's no safes in here, man. Just like she said."

"Bullshit!"

"Did you find one when you checked downstairs?" asked Will, with a little bite.

"Wait, what?" asked Chris. "You gettin' smart with me?"

The tone was not friendly or sarcastic. He'd stepped closer to Will, as if trying to figure out just how to respond to the insubordination.

"You got something to say to me, man?" asked Chris.

Reggie felt the tension between them. She saw Will swallow the lump in his throat. He was taller, broader than Chris. His mass was bigger, but he wasn't muscular. More... husky. He wore a short afro and goatee, both well-manicured. Reggie got the impression he didn't necessarily care about how he looked but cared more about how others saw his look. Something about him just screamed that he was always the kid trying to keep up with others.

"I'm just sayin' man... that there's nothing here. We're wasting our time. There's nothing here but this mir—"

"Man, fuck this mirror!"

Chris pushed his partner, raised his gun hand and squeezed the trigger. He fired seven shots, each in different areas of the mirror, each creating cracks and stress fractures in the glass. Reggie watched his head turn to her after he'd finished. His sneer was just as violent as his actions. Reggie met his gaze, shifted only briefly to look at the mirror before refocusing on him... and smiled.

The sound of the mirror repairing itself echoed in the empty room.

Both men turned to stare at the phenomenon, mouths agape. Silence echoed.

Then tiny nails tapped against the hardwood. Jasper pranced past Reggie, past the gunman and faced the mirror. He purred softly, but in the cavernous room, the vibration seemed to reverberate on the floors and walls. Without warning, Jasper leapt toward the mirror.

And then he was gone.

"What the—"

Chris' words were cut off at the sound of a roar.

A lion's roar.

And it was coming from the large feline now leaping from the mirror.

"So that's what he sees," whispered Reggie.

"Grandma! Did you see that?"

"See what, baby?"

"That," said Reggie, pointing at the mirror. "The woman. Me. Or someone that looked like me. Stepping out and like... I don't know... flying into me."

"I didn't see it, sweetheart."

Reggie felt defeated.

"But that's okay," began Mary, "because everybody sees what they need to see. Everybody sees what's most important for them to see. And only *they* can see it."

"Have you seen things?"

"Oh child, yes. Many things. And all those things made me who I am today. This mirror, baby, is special. It can make you into anything you want or need to be. If..."

A beat passed.

"If?" asked Reggie.

"If the person looking in the mirror is dedicated to the love of others. Service of others. And the protection of others. In other words... a person with a good heart. This mirror will show you your true self. And that, dear girl, is a superpower most people don't get."

Reggie stared into her grandmother's eyes and felt, more than heard, the truth of her words. Turning to look at the mirror, Reggie saw something etched into the bottom of the frame. It looked like a name. Crawling toward it, Reggie stretched out and traced the letters.

"What's this, Grandma?"

"That, baby girl, is our family name. The last name of the woman we're named after. The woman that gave this mirror its powers."

Reggie would not soon forget that name, or the meaning of her own.

***

Reggie watched as Chris scurried back in horror. Jasper had not only transformed into a lion, but a lion with a bloody mane. He looked as if he'd just fed on a wildebeest and was, in no way, satiated. Chris ran from the room, and Jasper followed, his roars echoing with the promise of carnage.

As they ran out, Reggie turned toward Will. Bottom lip quivering, whispers of the same words escaped.

"What the... what the... what the..."

"Easy Will," began Reggie, "calm down, take a few deep breaths and maybe you'll make it out of here alive."

Gunshots rang out. They were quickly followed by a roar and a scream. A scream of pain. A scream of terror. A very human scream.

"Your boy isn't doing too well with my kitty. If you want to escape his fate, drop that gun and any other weapons you may have. Jasper can be a little... sensitive and protective. And that's not when he's a lion the size of a rhino."

She said it as if it were a regular thing. As if Jasper transformed into a fierce lion every day. He didn't, but she was certainly pleased that he had today. Reggie searched for life in Will's eyes. She found only fear. Walking toward him, she lifted his head, called his name a few times, and when he didn't answer... she slapped him. Hard. Reggie could finally see awareness in his eyes.

"Do I have your attention?" she asked.

He nodded.

"Good. Now, as I was saying—"

Will dropped his gun, reached inside his coat, retrieved a knife, and dropped that, too. He *had* heard her. Even when practically catatonic. Following their trajectory to the floor, Reggie couldn't help but notice the wetness on his pants in the groin area, which led to a small but bright golden puddle on the floor.

"You're cleaning that shit up," she said.

"I... I... I'm sorry. I just... I don't even know what's going on," said Will, his hands on his head in terrified confusion.

"Well, what's going on is that you two morons came into this house looking for money, when, in fact, the only treasure is this mirror. My grandfather's money is in the bank, where most money is kept in the modern age by people who aren't criminals ready to flee the country at the sound of a siren or a hard knock on the door. This mirror, though? This mirror is one of a kind. Made by the lover of one of my ancestors. That ancestor used all her power to bless it."

"B-b-bless it?"

"Yep. Bless it. With words. With love. With magic," said Reggie, snapping her fingers and creating a burst of flame, causing Will to gasp and step back.

Reggie moved closer to the mirror and stared at her image. She thought back to the first time she saw it. The first time she sat with her grandmother and just stared at it. The time when the spirit of her ancestor stepped forward from the mirror and entered her body.

The first time she'd learned she was a witch.

"You see, this mirror has the power to bring out one's inner truth. It looks into their soul, learns who they really are, and brings that forth, so they can live their life in its most authentic form."

"But... I looked into it. I didn't see... anything. Just... my reflection."

"It's because of the conflict within you. Magic doesn't work without purity and purpose. You... you are living a life that others want you to live. You didn't want to do this today, did you?"

A beat passed before Will finally looked down and shook his head.

"You've been following this fool around for years... and for what? For him to push you around? Slap you? Threaten you? Threaten your family? Is that the life you want for yourself, Will? Is that truly who you are?"

Thud.

Thud.

Reggie turned to the sound of something hitting the walls beyond the room. The tap, tap, tap of razor-sharp claws on the hardwood floors announced a visitor arriving. Within seconds,

Jasper was backing into the room, dragging Chris by the criminal's foot. A foot that had seen better days.

Jasper stopped just short of the mirror and released Chris' foot. The hard impact on the floor seemed to jolt the man awake. His scream was blood-curdling. It was met with a roar, turning the scream into tears. Reggie watched as he tried to stand, but the struggle was real.

Real funny.

She stifled a laugh, which brought a look from Chris promising retribution, but it was a fleeting promise as Jasper bared his teeth and let out a growl.

"Help me up, fool," said Chris, looking at Will.

Reggie stared at Will, who, for a moment, stared back. After a beat though, he lowered his head, walked to his fallen partner, and helped the man to his feet.

"What the fuck!" said Chris, sniffing the air. "Is that piss? Did you piss yourself?"

The silence was deafening. Reggie felt sad for Will. Sad and embarrassed for him.

"You're not really in any condition to run things," began Reggie, "so why don't the two of you just back on out of here, and we'll forget this ever happened."

Her words were met with laughter.

"I'm not leaving without money, that mirror, and that thing dead," said Chris, pointing to Jasper.

"Dude," whispered Will.

"What?"

"Man, it's over. Let's just get out of here."

"What the hell you talkin' bout? It's over when I say it is."

Reggie stood, attentive and unbothered, next to Jasper, watching the two would-be thieves argue. She caught Will's gaze and gave a slight nod.

"Dude, look at this," said Will, turning Chris around to face the mirror. "What do you see?"

"A couple guys about to get paid if one of them acts right!"

"Look deeper," said Will.

There was silence for a while. Reggie stared ahead, beyond the two men, into the mirror. Even though she was a witch, even though the mirror was hers, she could not see another's images. But she could tell when they saw something. She could tell when something started to come into focus.

Chris Stone was having a moment.

"What the fu..."

"What do you see?" asked Will.

"It's like, a black pool, surrounded by fire, and... and..."

"And what?" asked Will.

"And... a bunch of hands coming out, reaching out, grabbing at something. It's like people are drowning. It's... it's..."

Reggie and Will stepped back at the first sound of Chris' scream. They stepped back further, his arms flailing about. His shriek was even louder than his encounter with Jasper.

"Get away from me! Get them off me! Help!" pleaded Chris.

Reggie's eyes widened as Chris rose into the air and floated toward the mirror. Chris continued to scream and struggle but kept floating toward the mirror. He reached out for help, but there was none. There was no salvation for him. A part of Reggie felt bad. She felt bad for him, for his soul, and for the torment he'd endure for eternity. She knew where he was headed.

Nevertheless, she smiled.

"Noooooooo!" screamed Chris as he began to enter the mirror, grabbing at the frame to avoid being sucked in completely.

And then he was gone.

"Wh-wh-what just happened?" asked Will.

"The mirror looked into his soul, and it saw darkness and

evil. And it took him to a place where those things exist... never to hurt anyone again."

Jasper roared.

"Holy shit!" screamed Will, clutching his chest.

The massive lion leapt into the mirror and simultaneously, a cat leapt from it. Jasper had returned to his true form. He pranced toward Reggie and rubbed up against her leg, purring. She knelt to pet him and looked up at Will.

"What are you going to do, Will? Because your next move will greatly impact mine."

As she spoke, she saw a flash of light in the mirror, and she knew. Her eyes had changed from hazel to gold. It happened when she called the power of her ancestor to the forefront. She was fully prepared to defend herself and her mirror, in this moment.

She'd hoped she wouldn't have to.

Will dropped to his knees. Tears fell from his cheeks. As he wept, Jasper walked slowly toward him. The cat brushed its body against Will's leg, purred, turned, and then sat next to the would-be thief.

"Jasper senses a change in you. Good call, Will. Good call," said Reggie.

Will nodded.

Reggie turned her gaze to the mirror, her eyes returned to normal. Will had turned his head too, and they stared together.

"Do you see anything?" asked Reggie.

"No."

"You will. One day," she said.

"What's that say?" asked Will as he crawled closer to the mirror.

Reggie watched as he traced the name etched into the bottom of the mirror frame.

"That's the name of my ancestor. She powered the mirror. She powers me."

They both stared at the name in silence.

Finally, Will spoke.

"Laveau."

A cool breeze flowed as the name echoed through the room.

PANTHER STARES BACK
By Evan Baughfman

I SLEEP FIFTEEN HOURS A DAY, WHICH DOESN'T GIVE me a whole lot of time to read. Though I always do manage to get those pages in, typically under moonlight. Night's when I'm most active, which probably seems strange to you since you're, you know, *people*, but that's just how I'm wired. You're bipedal for some reason, and I bet you've touched a bunch of dogs with your bare hands. So, try not to judge me, okay?

Besides, night's the best time for a book! Everybody in my house is snoozing by eleven-thirty, and that means no narrative interruptions, no sudden story stoppages. It's just me and the world an author's created and occasionally the crickets outside.

I'll drag whatever I'm reading behind some drapes, get comfy at a window, and bask in the celestial glow. See, my eyes are way better than yours, so sky's enough to illuminate even the tiniest fonts.

No doubt, by now, you're wondering how it's even possible for a cat to read. And, even if you're a self-proclaimed cat person, you probably have very little confidence in feline literacy. Well, that's because you don't know Chloe Davison.

Chloe's my best friend. She taught me to love books, to cuddle up with the written word.

She's also the one who named me "Purple". Yes, uh-huh, that's my name. It's a great moniker, don't deny it.

Story goes, Anna (Mom) and Robert (Dad) asked then three-year-old Chloe to name her new little kitten, and she had trouble figuring out who I was. So, they encouraged her to name me after something she already loved.

And that's why this black cat will forever be Purple.

Not Purp. Not Purpy. Not Purrple because you think puns are funny.

Purple, okay? Bet you wish your name were just as colorful as mine.

Anyhow, a year into my residency at the Davison family home, Chloe was excelling in preschool, learning how to read, how to write. Her parents were always consistent about reading to her, so that meant they shared stories with me too, since I was basically a magnet attached at the kid's side.

Problem was—and I hesitate to even call it a problem— Chloe's affinity for books accelerated at such a rate that she wanted to be reading every single moment of every single day. Only, Anna and Robert didn't have the time for constant read-alouds with their daughter. So, they came up with a wonderfully simple solution:

"Chloe, honey, why don't you practice reading on your own? You can read to Purple! I'm sure he'll enjoy it. You both will."

And they were right. During our reading sessions, Chloe and I grew even closer. Books tightened our bond. I was a captive audience, a student eager to learn. Because Chloe did something amazing as we read, something she probably picked up at school: she put her finger under each and every word as she said it to me. This guided my gaze and gradually expanded my vocabulary, as it did hers.

Back then, I'd fight off as much sleep as my biology allowed, because I wanted to stay on track with Chloe. The more she read, the more I absorbed. The more she grasped, the more I clung onto.

So, that dollhouse over by her bedroom closet? It didn't get very much use at all; we were reading so much. The structure became cobwebby, started resembling something we'd visit in October.

That mirror on Chloe's wall, the silvery, bejeweled one that Grandma gave her? Chloe would often pose in front of it, dressed up as a favorite literary character and then become that individual for a day.

Those stuffed animals I pushed to the floor every night? They turned into my classmates. Chloe diligently read to each and every one of us. I was her star pupil, of course, being the only student alive and with a brain.

Now, you have to understand, my vocal cords have never been able to do English, and Chloe's ears have never deciphered meows very well. Doesn't mean she wasn't a great teacher, okay? Everything I know today can be attributed to those formative years spent reading alongside my girl.

We went from cats in hats to curious primates. Then, we rode on magic school buses and climbed equally magical tree houses. From there, we gave ourselves goosebumps. After that, we discovered comics, and we swung high with Spider-Men, and solved mysteries with Batmen. We tried reading King in sixth grade, but admittedly most of *It* went over our heads.

In seventh grade, Chloe's bedroom library grew just like it did every year, but this time, new volumes went unread—unless I journeyed through them alone. See, seventh grade was also when Chloe got a laptop for her birthday, got a phone for good grades. Got a television mounted above her dresser on Christmas morning.

Chloe's a ninth-grader now, and yeah, she doesn't really

read anything of much substance anymore. Comments on social media and YouTube, maybe. Occasionally, she'll put the closed captions on T.V., but only if her parents ask her to "lower the volume, please."

Sure, I enjoy mindless cat videos just as much as you do. I've never turned my nose up at some good-natured clowning around. But my overall opinion of technology is... It's great, I guess, until you believe it's the only option around.

Sad to report, but recently it's like Chloe's completely forgotten about our past adventures together. Feels as if all I'll ever have are memories of long-ago fun. Because Chloe no longer appreciates or opens a book whenever I bring one to her. And she shoves me aside whenever I try to combat her addiction to the screen. Locks me outside of her room if I sit on her keyboard or wave my tail in front of Netflix.

These days, I have to consume whoever's on Robert's shelves. James Patterson. Dan Brown. Dean Koontz. Michaels Connelly and Crichton.

Anna's shelves aren't really my speed, you know? Jane Austen. The Brontë sisters. Diana Gabaldon. Nora Roberts. A talented bunch, but they don't really get my paws turning the pages.

What I wouldn't give for the works of Mo Willems to somehow reignite what Chloe and I once had...

"Purple, look at this."

Hey, school day's over, Chloe's returned home. She unzips her backpack and removes—*Am I dreaming?*—a book. The heavy tome drops beside me on her bed. Its title:

A Huge Book About Big Cats.

On its cover is a black feline, perched in a leafy tree canopy.

"That's you!" Chloe says. "Didn't know you were a model! Where do you find the time?" She giggles. Wish she'd do more of that when interacting with me these days.

Clearly, the cat isn't Purple. But I do see a bit of myself in his fur, in his eyes, in the way he embraces a sunbeam.

"A panther," Chloe explains. "Cool, right? I have to do an animal project for Science. I chose big cats. Lions and tigers and jaguars, oh my! Teacher made us all check out something from the library for 'research'. Why does she think we need books though, when everyone can just go on Google and find out stuff that way?" Chloe taps the *Big Cats* cover. "Thought you'd like that photo."

I do like it. I love it! What I don't love is Chloe's comment about Google. Is she really not going to read this book? I'm not the biggest fan of non-fiction, either, but still! *Google*? Blasphemy! We both know she's just going to distract herself by exploring other sites, the lure of the oceans-wide Internet right there at her fingertips.

Uh-oh. Chloe's already leaning against her pillows, laptop flipped open.

I meow, hoping to grab her attention. Meow again. When that proves to be fruitless, I squeeze under her arms, onto her lap, obstructing that glowing computer screen.

Yep! See? She's on Twitch, watching someone play video games! Knew it!

"Purple, no!"

Chloe lifts me away from her, and again places me beside *Big Cats*.

I stare at the panther. The panther stares back at me.

The book's almost a mirror. Good pieces of literature always are.

Hold on. Wait a second... Mirror... *Mirror*!

I know what I have to do.

I hop to the floor, travel to Chloe's closet. Door's ajar. I squeeze into the space, moving beneath dangling dresses, around stacks of teetering boxes, searching for...

Mirror, mirror... Where's that mirror...?

Way I heard it, Chloe's grandmother—Robert's mom— had been a witch. A really, really nice one, don't worry! Before she passed away, Grandma gave Chloe an enchanted mirror, a beloved family heirloom. (Just a side note here: I'm a descendant of Grandma's favorite cat, Gumdrop, which might help to explain why I'm so amazing and special.)

Okay, so, the mirror's magic works like this: when you look into the mirror, you become who/whatever you imagine yourself to be.

When we were younger, Chloe would morph into different figures inspired by the books we read. A knight in shining armor, a robot, or an astronaut, for example.

Literally.

I had the pleasure of being a unicorn, a baby Triceratops, and an octopus. And the great displeasure of once becoming a deciduous fern.

Literally.

When middle school hit, Chloe saw herself differently. On an almost-daily basis, she'd become something warty and grotesque: an orc, a troll, an ogre. The mirror had turned from a plaything into a cruel torture device. Thankfully, its magic always wore off after a dozen hours.

So, Anna swiftly detached the bewitched object from the wall and buried it deep inside her daughter's disorganized closet.

Which is where I'm currently hunting for the mirror. If I can just use the thing to transform into a panther, it should signal Chloe to focus on her studies, on her book. Especially when I snatch the laptop away with my mighty jaws.

Only, the closet's a tight squeeze, and my tail betrays me, sending an avalanche of random, abandoned treasures crashing my way. I yowl and barely make it out of there with all nine lives intact.

"What're you...? Purple, no!" Chloe has me in her hands. "Bad cat!"

Bad? *Bad*? I'm trying to do something for her own good!

Chloe doesn't realize this. She puts me in the hallway and slams her bedroom door shut.

Over the next seventeen hours, I sleep, eat, meow outside Chloe's room to no avail, sleep, read part of a Patterson novel, sleep, try a different Patterson novel, eat, sleep, start something by Koontz, wish I was reading about big cats instead, and sleep.

Next time I wake up, it's morning. Anna and Robert have gone to work. Chloe's gone to school. Her door is open.

A Huge Book About Big Cats is on the floor now. There is no bookmark indicating that any of the required information has made its way into Chloe's brain.

I return to the closet, still ajar. The mess I made yesterday is still a collision of chaos.

In the haphazard pile is a dented box missing its lid. The mirror rests inside the box, no gleam evident in the darkness.

I drag the box out into the sunny bedroom. The mirror sparkles, reflecting my whiskered face. I step away, not yet becoming something else.

See, before I commit to being a panther, I need to learn more about the animal, to make sure he's a good fit for me. Because years ago, I didn't do any research before becoming that fern, and it took quite a while to get all the chlorophyll out of my veins.

I dive into *A Huge Book About Big Cats*. Hours pass by as I float adrift in feline facts.

Did you know lions scavenge food and sometimes steal their meat from cheetahs?

Did you know tiger stripes are as distinct and unique as human fingerprints?

Did you know jaguars have the most powerful bite of all cats, relative to their size?

Once I finally finish the book, I'm ready to be more than me. I look into the mirror. I imagine a panther's muscular frame.

Seconds later, my body grows. My skull expands. My skin stretches.

Doesn't hurt, but I do get a little dizzy as I experience a little vertigo. Soon, however, the discomfort disappears.

And I feel great, standing taller, firmer.

My plan goes into motion. I remove the laptop from Chloe's room. I remove the television from her wall. I even remove her phone charger from its outlet.

I wait for my friend to arrive back home.

I'm large enough to reach doorknobs, so, in the backyard, I catch and eat a squirrel. I sleep. I read more Koontz. I sleep. I fail to catch or eat a sparrow. I re-enter Chloe's bedroom. I curl onto her sheets. I sleep.

"Purple, wake up!"

I yawn with my big mouth, displaying my big fangs. Night hasn't fallen yet.

Chloe stands over me. She says, "Congratulations on getting to Grandma's mirror. But what's the change for, huh?"

I step off her bed and nudge *A Huge Book About Big Cats* forward with a massive paw.

"Want to read that?" she asks. "Go ahead. But I don't need to, since I've got my—well, my phone's dead. But at least I have my..." She looks around the room. Realizes her technology is missing. "What did you do with all the...?"

Again, I nudge the book toward her.

She sighs, then smiles. "Clever cat. Show me what you did with my things after we read?"

I nuzzle her leg, showing her we have a deal.

Did you know panthers are merely leopards with black fur?

And did you know, pound for pound, leopards are the strongest of all cats, with the ability to carry more than their own body weight up into a tree?

Looking out the window, through sunshine, I hope that a strong wind doesn't suddenly decide to blow.

Chloe scratches me behind the ears and sits on the edge of her bed. I put my skull on her lap. She opens the book. Happy and comfy, I purr.

Well, I try to purr, but panthers can't actually vocalize in that way. My throat rumbles, emitting a gentle growl instead.

"What is *that*?" Chloe laughs and begins to read.

The rumble-growls continue.

You know what? Scratch what I said earlier, okay? (People don't have claws like me, but I think you realize that "scratching" is just a figure of speech anyhow, right?)

Because, yes, night's perfectly fine for reading.

But anytime with Chloe is the best time for a book.

THE DREAMWALKER
BY LARA YAMADA

The eighty-year-old's voice was impatient, and Alice paused before lowering her hands into the handbag. What had begun as an innocent indulgence had become an obsession.

"Here."

Alice reached around the soft belly, lifting the white and black cat, Little Woo, from the folded towel at the bottom. She placed him onto her grandmother's lap and watched the woman pretend to give the cat a few pats before setting it on the ground. The cat slunk around the legs of her chair before moving on to familiar corners with the inquisitive attentions of a traveler returning home to find their belongings slightly out of place.

With intense focus, the white-haired woman with the sun-kissed hands gripped the edge of the bed and followed the cat's movements around the room. While Grandmamma stared at the cat, Alice stared at her.

Her formerly stylish grandmother now believed an outfit was suitable if all the colors were aligned. Today it was a garish blue blouse, matching blue slacks that stopped at her knobby ankles, and bright blue slippers with a cotton poof on the top of the toes.

Little Woo arched his back and stretched out his legs. He was a good-natured fellow, and Alice held out her palm to him, cupped with a few fish-shaped treats. The cat never protested his clandestine ride to the Wise Oaks Elder Care Center, even compressed in a massive handbag that was better suited for a mother, toting necessities to support herself and six other humans.

Duty and empathy kept her coming back to Wise Oaks, although her grandmother wasn't particularly affectionate to either her or the cat. Since coming here, her grandmother had waved off Alice's attempts to embrace her and *faire la bise*—the customary cheek kisses—as they had always done since she was a child. Alice blamed it on the sudden move to the nursing home, when her uncle, a distant man she wasn't close to, had determined that Grandmamma's safety necessitated a permanent move to Wise Oaks, without discussing it with the rest of the family.

Wise Oaks took safety seriously. Too seriously.

"Nothing breakable allowed," the front desk attendant had told her on her first visit, her arms full of potted plants to brighten Grandmamma's new room. "No ceramic, no porcelain, no glass."

Alice was a rule follower, but after a long empty-handed walk through a maze of identical brown halls and scattered open community rooms filled with blank-eyed elders parked in front of windows facing gravel courtyards, Alice would have given her Grandmamma anything—anything, except the door codes required to exit through the locked doors of the Memory Care unit.

"How's the job?" her grandmother said, never taking her eyes off Little Woo.

"No travel this week, so I'm glad. Got to telework twice, which is always convenient, or I'd have to get the neighbor to walk Steven and Stormy."

"The dogs."

"Yes, the dogs."

For years, Alice had watched her grandmother age with a slow softening of the senses. She had leaned into frequent nostalgic conversations, trying to hold on to an identity that was becoming difficult to reconcile with the person she was becoming—the mother becoming the child, dependent on younger adults.

But things had changed since Grandmamma had come to Wise Oaks. The staff had provided Alice with a list of Grandmamma's current medications, and at least half of them had a side effect that involved, as the nurse put it, "the fuzzies and the foggies." Yet Alice could find no evidence of confusion in her grandmother. When the older woman wasn't absorbing Alice's tidbits of social information, it was only because she wasn't paying attention.

On the contrary, there was a new alertness in Grandmamma's entire presence that made Alice feel like the older woman wasn't the same person she'd always been. Her grandmother never talked about the past anymore and spent most of her visits asking about Alice and the news.

Grandmamma finally snapped her attention from the cat back to Alice.

"You seem sad. What's wrong?"

Alice readjusted her short red hair and clipped a loose bang back with a silver clip. She looked down at her boots. "Nothing. I just feel kind of out of it today. Work was stressful. I'd rather read books in bed and eat bacon straight from the oven and—" Alice trailed off. Grandmamma was no longer listening, her attention on Little Woo, and Alice fought her irritation.

Little Woo had hopped onto the tidy twin bed and made his way to the decorative pillows, where he stood on his back legs and pawed at the cheap plastic mirror over the headboard. Alice had offered, like she had most of the furnishings in the antiseptic room, to replace it with something of higher quality, but her grandmother had insisted on keeping it.

"Finally!" Grandmamma exclaimed and clapped her hands together. She moved with a snappiness that belied her age, angling around the bed to reach up and pluck the rectangular mirror off the wall and lay it flat on the duvet cover.

When she turned it over, it revealed a smaller mirror hidden on the other side. Crudely taped to the back with two strips of gray duct-tape, Alice could make out the shape of an ornate shield with a raised and textured border the color of burnt sienna. A few leaf clusters that embellished the left and right corners were broken off, but it was otherwise a beautiful antique.

Alice came closer. "What is that?"

"Something very important." The older woman looked at Alice with an intensity that made Alice feel uncomfortable.

"How did you get that in here?"

Little Woo slunk his way through Grandmamma's planted arms and sat on the cool glass surface. He pawed at his reflection behind spots of black mirror rot until Grandmamma yanked the mirror away from the back casing, tossing Little Woo to the side.

"Grandmamma!" Alice cried. She rushed over to scoop up the cat, and when she had turned, the blue-clad woman had taken the old mirror and locked herself into the ensuite bathroom.

There was a knock at the main door.

"It's Mark, one of the attendants. I'm here for timed medications."

"She's with a visitor, can you come back later?"

He didn't answer, but she heard keys moving against the doorknob. In a frantic dash, she bent over her chair and tried to stuff Little Woo in the handbag, but he was upset by the erratic movements and disappeared under the bed.

Alice straightened from her crouch on the floor as the door swung open.

The attendant wore maroon pants and a white shirt, and he had a silver cart with him, filled with various medical objects. "I have to check blood pressure, administer medication, and sanitize the space—and I've got ten other residents I have to finish within the hour. I hope you understand."

"She's occupied." Alice lifted her hand and gestured to the locked bathroom door.

"Sometimes she doesn't want to take the medicines. Could I suggest you wait outside for this part?" the man said.

"I'd rather stay." Alice clasped her hands behind her back and fought the urge to look down.

At the sound of an unfamiliar voice, Little Woo's head popped out from under the bed.

"Is that a cat? Did you bring that in here?"

A massive crash from the bathroom followed the man's accurate accusation, and he abandoned his interest in Little Woo to bang on the bathroom door.

"Orla? Open the door!"

Little Woo shot out from the room and headed down the hallway.

With a frustrated cry, Alice rose from the carpet. She made a last-ditch effort to grab him, and instead of an armful of cat, she ended up with a knee-full of rugburn.

Mark shot her a glare and continued his barrage on the door.

"I'm coming in!" He gave his keyring an aggressive shake

before fumbling through them, lifting a long shepherd's hook key to the knob.

Alice was torn—she should stay and help Grandmamma? But this man and his drug cart had subjected her grandmother on the daily. Little Woo was her responsibility, and she had to protect him.

"Grandmamma, I'll be right back!" she shouted and ran after the cat.

Soledane was free.

His mouth was dry, and his pupils were constantly in flux, rapidly absorbing the light coming from the light fixtures over the green sink.

He looked down at the old woman on the ground. Her head was tilted against a pink wicker laundry basket, and her legs were folded in a way that would make her knees ache for days.

He hated this bathroom, but it paled compared to how he felt being trapped in the body of an elderly person. And not just any elder—one who'd been equally trapped for the crimes of forgetfulness and fragility.

With unsteady movements, he ducked behind the plastic shower curtain and lowered himself to sit on the shower bench. He prayed the attendant wouldn't think to check it. He didn't have the strength to fight anyone.

The door swung open. Holding himself still, Soledane listened to the sounds of the man's efforts to revive Orla.

"Chris, get the head attendant. It's Orla Caine. She's in the bathroom, covered in glass. Some sort of mirror. No idea how she got it." A pause. "You know how she is. Didn't get it from me," the man growled into his radio. "Probably that grand-daughter. She just doesn't get it. Has no *clue* what it takes to work here. I'm not going to finish the other residents. Yeah. Okay."

Through a gap in the curtain, he watched Mark carry Orla out of the bathroom and lay her on her side.

Soledane looked down at the shirt and pants he was wearing when he'd been caught. Thankfully, it wasn't one of the traditional outfits, just a gray shirt, tan pants, and black shoes.

He lifted a hand to his chest and felt the heartbeat thumping there, readjusting to the hormones and testosterone unique to himself—the body of a twenty-year-old male.

Soledane gave himself just long enough to breathe.

The final act to free himself from Orla's body was simple. He just had to look into an aged mirror when the mirror's energy lines were strongest, find himself inside the gaze of a stranger's eyes, and will himself back into his own existence.

It was no small feat to hold onto his authentic self when it was also entwined with someone else's. In a stranger's body, his senses were muted, and he could have easily lost himself.

"Are you coming? I'm going to start CPR. If I crack a rib, I'm not responsible—okay—here it goes." The attendant set his phone on the ground and bent over Orla's motionless body.

Soledane forced himself into motion. He tiptoed around the shattered mirror glass spread out over the bathroom tiles and sidled through a mere fifteen inches of open door, nearly choking on the smell of floral perfume coming from the hall. He put his nose against his shoulder and forced down a cough.

When he was right behind Mark's back, he held his breath. The cheap mirror that had hidden the old one had been laid aside, but he worried that the late afternoon light could shift the shadows as he passed.

Fortunately, Mark was so engrossed in his revival efforts that he didn't notice the interloper's slow steps against the wall. When Soledane was in the hallway, he relaxed his shoulders and tried to act inconspicuous.

Alice.

He followed the sounds of commotion,"A cat! Let me hold it!" to shouts of outrage, "What the heck is that thing doin' here?" and absorbed the familiar voices with conflicted feelings. As his long legs carried him forward across a stretch of hallway lined with pictures of watercolor flowers, waves of relief washed over him.

No more trivia games. No more daytime movies. No more communal meals taken elbow to elbow with the companions that had kept him company for the past six months, eager for the highlight of their day to be placed on the seasonal placemats in front of them.

As a dreamwalker, he was no stranger to the thoughts and emotions of all ages. It pained him that the golden ticket required to walk out of this cage was to be youthful and able-bodied. It wasn't a ticket anyone could hold onto.

"Herbst. Harper. Geherty. Greene. Egland."

Soledane didn't need to look at the name placards to know each of the people who lived behind those doors. He knew that behind every fake orchid, plastic wreath and resin garden animal propped outside was a human being who felt heartbreaking feelings of abandonment.

A few enjoyed the community living, but most felt like their families had thrown them away. And even if they couldn't lay blame on someone else, there were the dreams they had no more time or ability to realize, and the futility of "Get Well" cards for physical complications that had become permanent.

His eldest brother probably hoped his entrapment would discourage him from acting on the gifts he'd inherited, but his experience had only strengthened his resolve and empathy. His time as Orla Caine at Wise Oaks had shaken him to his core, and he would never forget it.

In dreams, he sat with strangers and spoke to them. In dreams, he could show people what their hearts wanted and what their minds lacked the imagination to see.

His gift was to bring hope. It was needed and wanted, and he would never stop.

In Orla Caine's body, Soledane had initially approached his nursing home companions the way he did when he visited someone in a dream. He sat with them and tried to draw out their thoughts. He spent time listening to them as they spoke of their dreams.

As a dreamwalker, he was a transient visitor. He counted on the freedom of leaving the canvas of mental emotions he'd stepped into, especially when the power of creating visions and dreams failed. Not every dream ended well.

But as a trapped participant in the same life as the nursing home residents, it became too much for him to handle when the months passed, and he was still stuck in the same place. He was as powerless as they were, and he began to distance himself mentally and emotionally. It was vastly different approaching others from a place of power than coming from the same place of vulnerability, and he regretted he wasn't strong enough to have made a significant impact to any of them in his short time here.

"Ma'am, you need to leave."

The sharp voice broke his thoughts. Soledane walked faster, rounding the corner as the head attendant came head-to-head with Alice.

"I understand what she asked of you, but our residents have many requests that shouldn't be granted, for their safety, and the safety of others. Unfortunately, your visitation rights are suspended for two weeks."

"But I'm her only visitor!"

He felt another twinge of guilt. It was his fault Orla had lost friends. He shared her thoughts and memories, but his own consciousness dominated most interactions. He couldn't feign the familiarity or interest her friends required to keep coming back to the cage they themselves were dangerously close to being caught in.

"I need to let her know. She'll be upset if I don't—"

"We'll let her know," the nurse snapped, cutting Alice off. "Thomas, escort our guest out the back."

"I don't have my keys!" Alice complained. "I don't even have my phone."

Before he could intervene, a voice chimed by his side, and he looked down.

"Wow!" It was one of the younger residents, only in her sixties—Crazy Abby. "You're a looker. Where'd you come from? Don't tell me." She held up two hands and shook her head. "I don't want to get involved. It'll be a story I won't be able to keep to myself."

"I..." Soledane stalled. He didn't know how to behave anymore. And he had completely forgotten his cover story. "I —I'm visiting—"

"Don't lie to me, son. But you know where to come if you need help. Your kind always does." She turned abruptly, smacking her cane against the fish-tank glass.

"Ms. Walker!" The head attendant's attention had been diverted.

Soledane's eyes followed the bobbing motion of a white angelfish, belly-up at the surface of the clear tank. Across the other side of the tank, his eyes found Alice.

She had become a familiar and comforting face to him. No longer restricted by the general blur of Orla's sun-damaged eyes, Soledane looked at her, taking in the details with renewed interest. Her wide-spaced eyes and the smattering of acne along her chin made her appear juvenile, although he knew she was twenty-five. Her expression was often stern, which fitted her personality, although it contrasted with the bright and colorful clothes she wore.

"Excuse me," Soledane called out. She didn't seem to hear him.

He walked around the fish tank and waved again.

"I could hold the cat if you need to get your things," he tried again.

She ignored him.

He realized his large frame could seem intimidating to some, but he usually attracted at least an acknowledgement.

"Alice?" he ventured. He was a foot away.

But only the cat had fixed its massive gray eyes on him.

Most animals were sensitive to the supernatural, but cats tended to act on the curiosity that supernatural objects tempted them with.

When his brother blocked his natural path to return to his body after a dreamwalk, he had to find an alternative way. The mirror that had freed him had absorbed the energy of dozens of humans and hundreds of passing moments. Today, the mirror's energy crossed lines with the Earth's energy, making it ready to use.

Like so many mysterious things that people mistakenly labeled "magic," it was simply another crossing of energies, and it was neither predictable nor controllable.

The cat had sensed the invisible effect where Soledane could not.

The realization hit him. In a sudden jolt, Soledane reached out for Alice's hand and watched it pass through her palm without connecting.

In his eagerness to be free of Orla Caine's body, he had disregarded the basic principles of science. The energy required to release a soul couldn't conjure up physical mass.

Soledane felt like a fool. A soul without a body was little

more than a ghost, a spirit whose physical form had perished. For some, it was a matter of days—for others, it was hours.

There was only one solution.

Until he found his comatose body in northern Washington, thousands of miles from Wise Oaks Nursing Home in Ohio, he would have to share space with a soul one more time.

"We'll call you by the end of the week." The woman shook Alice's hand and offered a brief smile. Alice looked down at the resume she had set on the desk, grateful she'd thought to print extra copies. The woman had asked for five copies, one for each of the five interviewers.

At home, Alice changed out of her gray interview suit and hung it on the wooden hanger. A few strands of Little Woo's fur still clung to the shoulder of the black suit next to it, and she pulled a white strand off to stare at it. The last time she'd worn the black suit was five years ago. Little Woo had pressed his head against her neck and let her hold onto him for a long time, hours after the last guest had left from her mother's funeral.

Without meaning to, her eyes filled with tears, and she had a good cry. The tears she didn't want to cry over Grandmamma and the tears she no longer cried for her mother, she let fall for Little Woo.

A few pats with the concealer brush brought her face back from lobster red to light beige. She drank a few glasses of cold water and slid golden aviators over her puffy eyes.

Little Woo had been missing for a month. After the embarrassing incident at the nursing home, things seemed better with Grandmamma. The older woman had suffered a few lacerations to the arms and hands from her fumble with the antique mirror and minor rib bruising from a moment of

CPR. Although Grandmamma had offered no explanation for that day, a sweetness and gentleness had returned to her motions that Alice had missed. But while things were more affectionate with Grandmamma, the opposite happened with Little Woo.

Little Woo began spending more time outside and refused to sleep at the foot of her bed. When she caught him in a sneak attack on a backyard bird, she tied a bell on his collar and tried to keep him inside. But one evening, he never came back.

Weeks of a Lost Cat poster hadn't led to any serious calls until one came from the apologetic head attendant at Wise Oaks.

"I'm so sorry. Your grandmother has COVID and is in critical care at the main hospital."

After a two-week quarantine from visitors, Grandmamma stayed on as a long-term patient with additional complications. For Alice, it wasn't much different from her visits to Wise Oaks, except Grandmamma spent more time asleep or unable to speak from the breathing device on her face.

Alice spent as much time as she could afford sitting by Grandmamma's small medical bed, reading out loud from her grandmother's favorite historical fiction novels. She blew through her vacation days and her sick days. Reluctantly, she'd given her two week's notice when her boss firmly requested her to accompany the staff on a conference out of state.

Hence the interview for a new job. With the interview fresh in her mind, Alice stopped promptly at yellow lights and hovered just above the speed limit, resisting the pressure of the impatient trucks and vans tailing close behind. Newly unemployed, she couldn't afford any speeding tickets. She let out a breath when she pulled into the hospital parking lot, spending a few more minutes collecting her thoughts. When that didn't work, she turned on a deep breathing exercise from a phone app and closed to her eyes to concentrate.

"I'm going to be okay. I'm going to be okay." She repeated the propaganda out loud, trying to believe it. Opening her eyes, she nearly choked on her words when she saw a man sitting on a bench petting a cat. She darted out of the driver's seat and strode towards them.

The cat looked relaxed and comfortable, stretched across the man's lap. Its eyes were half closed, and its fur had been flattened on the top of its head where the man's fingers continued to stroke the same place.

Her heart nearly leapt out of her chest. White and black fur, the small diamond shape across the forehead, the dip on the left ear—all the familiar markings of her dearest pet.

"Little Woo?" Alice cried.

"Hello. Is this your cat?"

The man's deep voice surprised her, and she did a double take.

He was young, his sleek black hair flowing around his long face and his shoulders. She instinctively touched her own rough red hair. He had thick eyebrows, a long straight nose, and high cheekbones she would have killed for. He wore simple dark jeans and a green shirt covered with white cat fur.

"Little Woo?" she whispered again, kneeling next to the man's knees. She reached out, and the cat tensed, then relaxed and let her tuck him into her elbows and forearms.

Her eyes smarted with tears for a second time that hour, and she buried her face into his soft fur. He smelled good, like someone had recently bathed him.

"Did you find him?"

"I'd say he found me."

The man rose from the bench, and Alice realized the clean smell of the cat's fur was also coming from his clothes. It was a mix of cologne and dryer sheets, but before she could press for more details, he pointed to the hospital door.

"I think you should go in. I'll hold him until you get back."

Alice stalled, holding Little Woo's warmth in her bare arms, cradling his comforting weight. Her heart felt fuller than it had in weeks. She wanted to stay with him, with Little Woo, but she knew Grandmamma was waiting—she was already an hour later than she usually visited.

"He won't run away," the man added quietly. "I'll wait here."

Alice relented with a soft acknowledgement.

"Thank you."

The young man reached for Little Woo; for a moment their forearms touched, and they held the cat together. Then the pressure of the little paws was gone, and Little Woo was back in the protective cage of the stranger's tan arms.

The swoosh of the sliding doors, and the blast of cold air-conditioning against Alice's neck made her shiver. Looking over her shoulder, she stared at the man who had reseated himself on the bench with Little Woo back on his lap.

It's the handsome ones you have to watch out for, Grandmamma's voice warned her. She should have gotten his name. Better yet, she should have taken Little Woo home, then come back. She wasn't thinking clearly and wondered what had possessed her to willingly follow his suggestions. His directness and confidence disarmed her, and she made a mental note to imitate his style in her next interview.

All of her thoughts came crashing to a halt when she rounded the corner.

A familiar nurse practitioner leaned over the front desk, speaking with the check-in staff. When the woman turned to Alice, she stepped forward as if she'd been waiting.

"You're here for your grandmother." The woman said it as a statement. "Please come with me."

The woman's voice was kind. Sympathetic.

A doctor came to the room seconds after Alice sat down. As he began to speak, the shock spread over her limbs until she was so frozen, she couldn't even feel her face. She held herself in rigid stillness, unable to accept the small box the nurse offered.

When her eyes could finally blink past her tears, she looked down. Perched on top of Grandmamma's neatly folded and stacked hospital possessions was a single white envelope.

Soledane felt terrible. He'd come back as soon as he could, but it was too late.

The journey back to his home was harrowing, and he wondered often what would happen if he died in the cat's little body. He didn't have the strength, or the mirror required to dreamwalk to another human, so he had chosen Little Woo to get out of the nursing home.

He would have chosen to become a bird for the long journey home, but at that point, his spiritual energy had been depleted, and he was stuck. He'd waited until he'd mastered catching small prey and then began his trek back to the North.

There were too many close calls with loose dogs and swooping hawks by day and owls by night. But he had kept going with dogged determination, sensing which humans could be trusted. He got lucky when he slid into the backseat of a trucker headed to Washington state.

Lifting himself from the cat's soul had been excruciatingly painful. With the cat's instincts, he'd been able to see the tangible lines of energy hovering over his bedridden body in the hospital. He'd waited until the energy lines ran thick and pulsing with faint light and then used it the same way he'd done with Orla, staring into the reflection of a metal hospital tray. Because he was lifting himself from an animal, the energy lines didn't have to be as strong as the ones generated by the antique mirror.

This time, he'd made sure it was real. He'd plucked every IV cord from his wrists and veins and rose to touch the first person he'd seen. It was a night nurse, and she had screamed when she saw him standing at the end of a dim hallway, hovering with his long, greasy hair and a white hospital gown.

Now that he'd returned twice, Soledane knew he could do it again.

It had been a stroke of luck he'd found the right book at Wise Oaks he'd needed to glean the bit of hidden knowledge about the mirror. He might never have found a way to circumvent the block his brother had placed on his energy line if a particular staff member at Wise Oaks hadn't set up a collaboration with the community for donations.

True to its name, Wise Oaks was the last stop for thrift store and library cast-offs. With an abundance of time and patience, he'd combed through hundreds of donated books crammed inside of musty boxes until he'd found a book detailed with unsubstantiated energy theories. It had been written eighty years ago, or he would have endeavored to thank the author for giving him a path to freedom.

As he'd suspected, his parents had no idea what had happened to him. His three brothers had made a pact not to tell their parents of their different abilities, and when Soledane had made the reconnection with his body on a Saturday morning at dawn, he'd feared his oldest brother could sense his return and journey to the hospital to confront him.

So, he'd contacted his parents, and his mother had immediately taken him to a medicinal healer who had heaped dozens of herbal supplements into his hands and told him how to avoid a weak body.

"You need to get stronger, so you don't get ill again."

His father had agreed with the treatment plan, and he had hovered around him until he was alone and able to book a flight back to Ohio. He felt an urgent weight on his heart, but it cleared the moment he stepped on the plane.

"Everything alright?"

The flight attendant who had taken his ticket and directed him to the left aisle noticed the falter and the hand he threw out to grip the closest headrest. The relief was sudden and fleeting before a new heaviness settled into his soul-sorrow for Alice.

Orla Caine had passed from the realm of the living to the land of the risen.

Soledane didn't know what she'd shared with her granddaughter before her passing, so while on the plane, he had put down on paper everything he knew.

Every piece of wisdom she'd carried in her mind, every anecdote and piece of advice she'd especially marked to share with Alice, Soledane wrote it down. It was nearly twenty pages when he'd finished, and he brought it to Orla Caine's hospital bed just before Alice had arrived.

Soledane regretted he didn't have more time.

"I'll be back when I get things sorted out," he told Little Woo. "Otherwise, my brother might just stick me back here as Crazy Abby."

He petted the cat a few more times before he lifted his chin to stare at the floating clouds. The sky was the perfect blue, the air warm, and the distant murmur of voices wove through the opening and closing hospital doors.

He inhaled deeply and felt the lingering presence of Orla Caine. She was there as surely as the warmth of the sun and the fragrant honeysuckle bushes near the benches.

His lips parted, and he spoke quietly.

"She knows everything. If there's something I've forgotten, I'll tell her later."

The breeze moved stronger against his bare skin, and a bird flew out from the shrubs, spiraling towards the bright sun. He thought of the final page he'd written against the open tray table of the plane seat.

"The way to stay young forever is to stay connected. Talk to all people, especially people who are smarter than you. If you're old, that means the young people. If you're young, that means the old people. Be curious. Love others. Never forget—people are magic."

Even with his gift of dreamwalking and everything he knew about different energies; the most powerful magic was always the simplest one.

Connectedness.

Soledane had thought he'd held onto his sense of self when he was trapped in Orla Caine's body due to sheer willpower and Alice's reminders of the outside world. He understood now that he was wrong.

He had survived the joint-soul experience because the other soul hadn't overtaken him. Orla had shared her space and consciousness with him until he'd found a way out.

Between the two of them, her eighty years of soul strength could have easily overpowered his mere twenty—the soul and the body were completely different sources of strength. He was ashamed to admit he had greatly underestimated her power because it had been disguised within a fragile body.

He still had so much to learn.

He could come back for Alice when things were safer with his brother. From the few chances he'd had to step into his brother's dreams, his oldest brother's powers were far more dangerous than he'd realized.

"Take care of her," Soledane murmured to the cat. With a last pat, he timed his final departure as Alice approached the glass doors. Even from a distance, he could see the devastation on her face. He trusted the nurse had given her the letter. He set the cat down to step into the taxi when she was steps away.

He was afraid of what he'd reveal if he stayed long enough to pass her the cat.

He watched her scoop him into her arms as the taxi turned the corner and tried to quell his nerves.

Alice wasn't a dreamwalker, but she'd been in his dreams since her first visit to Wise Oaks.

Now he would become a part of hers.

Off Balance

By Kari Shuey & Angela Perry

A low growl rose from the back seat of the Tacoma.

"Aww, it's okay, Cleo." Erin turned in the passenger seat and waggled a finger at the cat carrier. "For a kitten, she sure can sound scary when she wants to. I think she's sick of being cooped up."

Mathias adjusted his sunglasses and focused on breathing through his mouth. Cleo wasn't the only one ready to claw her way out of the truck. The sweet smell of Erin's blood crept into his nostrils, coaxing darkness from the edges of his vision. His fangs prickled at his gums.

A two-hour car trip with Erin had seemed doable—until it started raining. Now he was trapped in a confined space with her, and the demon in his skull wanted nothing more than to tear her throat out.

"Matt, there it is!" Erin gave a little bounce. "That's the Belfast exit."

Mathias squinted through the pounding rain. To his right, a road branched from the highway. He eased around the turn, wheels splashing through standing water. With Erin chirping directions in his ear, he steered the truck through the town until they reached a modest duplex.

"It's the one with the blue door." Erin tapped her phone, closing the navigation app, and sighed. "Wow, it's wet. Oh well, better get it over with."

She dove into the downpour, leaving Mathias to follow with Cleo. The rain sluiced over him like a chilly shower. He took off his sunglasses, lifted his face to the deluge, and smiled. People said water washed away sins. It washed away innocence too. No bitter or sweet blood smells. Only the cleansing neutrality of nature.

Cleo hissed from inside the carrier.

Mathias shook water from his eyes and peered through an airhole into the enclosed space. "You're fine. You can't be getting more than a few drops in there."

He caught up to Erin on the doorstep. She leaned against the doorbell, her honey-colored hair dark and streaming into her face. Raindrops gathered on her glasses, nearly obscuring her blue eyes. The door swung open, and she didn't wait for an invitation. Mathias followed on her heels, dripping water onto the carpeted floor.

"Michelle, it's so good to see you!" Erin threw her arms around the elfin woman hovering next to the door. "Oh, sorry. I'm soaked."

She stepped back, giving Mathias his first good look at Michelle since she'd left Felmond. His heart stuttered, and he swallowed hard. If possible, she was even more beautiful. Barrettes winked in her blond pixie cut, which had grown shaggier. Her cheekbones were more pronounced, and her green eyes carried a new depth.

Suffering had done that. He winced and dropped his gaze. He'd never forgive himself for not being there to protect her. The gunshot had almost taken her from him. The way he'd slaughtered the gunman before her eyes had finished the job.

She might not remember it, but he could tell from her furtive expression that his presence still set her on edge.

"Hi Matt." Her tentative smile didn't reach her eyes. "Thanks for coming all this way to help." She glanced at the cat carrier, and her smile turned genuine. "You brought Cleo?"

Erin giggled. "Matt doesn't trust his roommate to take care of her, even overnight."

"That's okay! She's always welcome." Michelle squatted in front of the carrier, fiddled with the latch, and swung the door open.

As though she hadn't been demanding to be released minutes earlier, Cleo sauntered into the room, flicking water from her paws with dainty disgust. The rest of her black fur was dry and gleaming. Mathias rolled his eyes. Typical.

Michelle swept the kitten into her arms, cooing. Cleo permitted the attention, winking her blue eye and glaring at Mathias with the green one.

"I'd offer you towels, but I already took them to my mom's." Michelle gestured at the nearly empty room. "All that's left are the big things I couldn't move myself."

"Don't worry about it. We'll just get wet again." Erin wiped her glasses on a dry corner of her shirt. "How's your mom doing?"

Michelle shrugged, her face a careful blank. "As well as can be expected. Her lupus is bad. All the stress when they killed my dad, and after what happened to me..." She placed Cleo on the floor and ran a hand over the kitten's soft fur, avoiding their gazes. "My brother and sister help out, but teens have social lives, you know? I need to be there."

Mathias exchanged a look with Erin. It was obvious Michelle felt responsible for her mother's condition. Even after a hundred years, he still didn't know the right thing to say in these situations. Michelle's pulse thumped faintly in his ears. The scent of her blood, which had always been light, was almost undetectable now. His demon barely noticed her. He longed to reach out to her, yet the emotional distance between them couldn't be wider.

Cleo saved him by bolting down the hallway. Her sudden movement made everyone jump, breaking the awkward silence.

Michelle pressed a hand to her chest and gave a breathless laugh. "I forgot how much fun cats are."

"Crazy, more like." Mathias peered after her. "She can't get into anything back there, can she?"

"Well..." Michelle grimaced. "I have some things stacked in the bedroom. Maybe I'd better—"

"I'll get her." Seizing the opportunity to escape, he bounded down the short hallway.

Like the living room, the bedroom was almost empty. A mattress and dismantled bed frame rested against the far wall. The drawers had been pulled out of a low dresser and piled beneath the window. Cleo stood in the middle of the room, staring at a flat object covered in a quilt leaning against the dresser.

"What are you so interested in?"

The kitten ignored him, as usual. Mathias shook his head. Here he was, a creature of nightmares, getting bullied by a cat. One corner of his mouth quirked up. She kept him humble.

He spun in a slow circle, taking in the room. Even mostly empty, it held traces of *her*. The light, sweet scent of her blood. The faint perfume of her shampoo. The pale rose paint on the wall, streaked with wan light and shadow from the rain running down the window. A twinge ran through his chest, and he closed his eyes.

A loud yowl echoed through the room. Mathias's eyes sprang open, and he dropped into a defensive crouch. Even with his enhanced reflexes, he caught only a glimpse of Cleo's black tail disappearing through the doorway. The quilt lay crumpled on the floor next to an oval mirror in an ornate frame.

With a snort, Mathias relaxed, and stood upright. Cleo's reflection had scared her. Crazy wasn't a strong enough word for that cat.

He squatted in front of the mirror, admiring the delicately carved scrollwork on the frame. It was polished but worn. An antique. He didn't know much about woodwork, but he'd guess the seventeenth century—even older than he was. The glass had a bright sheen, almost a glow. It reflected his damp, tousled dark hair and hazel eyes with such precision that, for an instant, it seemed more real than he did.

"Matt? Everything okay back there?" Erin's voice drifted from the living room. "Cleo's freaking out."

Mathias opened his mouth to reply and froze. Something moved in the mirror. Black smoke twined around his reflection's head and shoulders. Mathias shifted his eyes to the side, but the smoke wasn't visible outside the silvered glass.

A pulse of energy surged from the mirror. Red eyes opened in the smoke, and an enormous mouth filled with razor sharp fangs gaped open. Mathias grabbed the quilt and threw it over the mirror, shrouding the horror in front of him.

"Matt?"

He whirled, his breath caught in his throat. Michelle stood in the doorway, a faint crease between her eyes. Had she seen... whatever that was?

"Cleo's on top of the bookcase." Michelle's voice was calm, if a little worried. She couldn't have seen it. "Erin's trying to coax her down. What happened?"

Mathias fought to keep his voice steady. "She knocked the quilt off your mirror, and scared herself, that's all." If Cleo had seen what he had, Erin wouldn't get her down anytime soon.

Michelle let loose a peal of laughter. "Leave it to a cat to be afraid of her own reflection."

Right. Leave it to the cat. "It's a beautiful mirror. It almost has a glow, doesn't it?"

"Glow?" Michelle tilted her head. "I don't remember that. It's probably just the weird lighting in here."

Before he could stop her, she pulled the quilt free. Mathias pressed against the wall, staying out of the field of reflection. Nothing happened. Michelle's image appeared to be perfectly normal. She bent to stare into the mirror, rubbed at a faint spot on the glass, then turned her head and raised an eyebrow.

He shrugged. "Must have been the light."

"It belonged to my grandmother." She ran a loving finger over the carvings. "She always said it was special and made me promise to give it to my daughter someday. It's been passed down through the women in my family for generations. Did you see the poem engraved on this little plate?"

Mathias mutely shook his head. Her voice took on a singsong quality as she read the inscription.

Herein lies the truth
But stare not overlong
Ere strong becomes weak
And weak becomes strong

A thrum of energy rippled from the mirror, but Michelle didn't react.

"I figure it means you shouldn't be conceited, or something like that." A gentle smile tugged at her lips. "Maybe I won't put it in storage. I'll hang it in my old bedroom where it belongs."

Mathias cleared his throat. "That's... a thought."

He did his best to avoid the bedroom for the rest of the afternoon. Cleo concurred, perching on top of the bookcase until she was forced to jump down when they moved it. She retreated to the coat closet and growled at anyone who tried to entice her out.

It took several trips with the Tacoma to move the furniture to the storage unit. Luckily, the rain lessened to a light drizzle, so nothing got completely soaked. Each time they returned to the duplex for another load, the weird energy Mathais had felt from the mirror grew stronger, until it practically rattled his teeth.

"Whew." Erin slammed the tailgate and pushed her damp hair from her forehead. "I wasn't sure we'd finish tonight. That's the last of it, right?"

"We still need the mirror." Michelle eyed the load. "I bet I can fit it into the back seat of my car. Want to help me carry it out, Matt?"

He gritted his teeth. He couldn't think of anything he wanted less. "Sure."

Erin gave them a thumbs up. "I'll see if I can get little miss grumpy puss into her carrier without losing a finger."

Mathias trailed after Michelle down the hallway. A burnt metallic scent tickled his nostrils. His ears rang with the power resonating through the bedroom, and a strong greenish light glowed through the checkered quilt.

"Ouch." Michelle rubbed her temple. "Change in atmospheric pressure. Storms get my ears every time."

"Michelle, wait." Mathias grabbed her arm. "We should talk about—"

"About what happened at the hospital. I know." She turned and looked up at him. "I didn't mean to hurt you, Matt."

"No, I—"

She raised her hand. "Please let me finish. I've been trying to find the nerve to say this all afternoon. I'm so sorry for the way things ended between us. You saved my life, and I pushed you away. You reminded me of something I wanted to forget. It wasn't fair. And—" She took a deep breath. "It's not fair to ask this either, but... I'd like a second chance with you."

Her green eyes captured his and drew him in. The power in the room faded into the background. A century of loneliness crashed over him, driving the air from his lungs. Could he risk it? He brushed her cheek with trembling fingers. She'd given him a glimpse of happiness he'd thought forever lost to him.

But nothing had changed. He was still a monster. If the demon defeated his control, even for a moment, she could become his next victim. He wasn't simply risking his heart. He was risking her life.

His voice came out as a broken whisper. "I can't—"

She turned away, brushing at her eyes. "It's okay. I understand."

The tears in her voice stabbed him through the heart. No, she didn't. She couldn't ever understand.

A scream reverberated from the front room. Michelle's head jerked around, and they stared wide-eyed at each other for a heartbeat. Then Mathias charged down the hallway, Michelle at his heels.

The front door hung from one hinge, letting in the rain and darkness. Erin lay sprawled on the floor by the coat closet, the cat carrier on its side. A woman with long, straight ebony hair stood over her. She lifted her face, revealing solid black eyes.

"Sleep." She waved a negligent hand in their direction.

Michelle crumpled. Mathias caught her as she fell and eased her to the carpet. Then he surged to his feet, deep crimson washing across his vision.

"What did you do?" His fangs distorted the words. "Undo it. Now."

The woman blinked at him. "Did she send another?" She took a deep breath and wrinkled her nose. "No, you can't be one of hers. You reek of guilty blood. How *pathetic*."

Faster than his eyes could track, she was in front of him, her fingers curled around his throat. Her scent, a sweet decay, wormed its way into his lungs, and he choked. The demon in his head snarled, forcing its awareness on him. Predator. Rival. Kill her.

"Kill me?" The woman threw her head back and roared with laughter. "I'd love to see you try."

With a flick of her arm, she threw Mathias across the living room. He crashed through the drywall into the kitchen. He rebounded to his feet, bits of plaster flying in all directions. The rational part of his mind made him hesitate. Another vampire. He'd only fought one other of his kind before, and he'd had the drop on him. This woman was far more powerful than he was. He should get Erin, Michelle, and Cleo out of here.

The vampire quirked an eyebrow at him, bared her fangs in a smile, and disappeared down the hallway. The mirror. Of course, the power must have drawn her here. Its energy thudded through the walls, vibrating the entire house. Whatever the mirror was, it was too powerful to fall into the hands of a creature like that.

He pulled his folding karambit from his pocket and snapped the blade open. All he had to do was catch her unawares. Using every ounce of his stealth, he crept down the hallway after her.

Green light edged her silhouette as she stood before the covered mirror. Its rippling energy made it hard for him to focus. He could only hope it was having the same effect on her senses. He lunged, driving the curved blade into the side of her neck. She howled and whirled on him.

"Stupid, filthy, wretched little creature." She grabbed his throat and slammed him against the wall. With her free hand, she pulled a sharp wooden stake from her coat. "That was your last mistake."

A small black shape sprang from the shadows. Yowling, Cleo clawed and bit at the woman's hand. Her hand twitched, and she dropped the stake, though Mathias suspected it was more from surprise than pain. She lifted her arm to eye level, staring at the clinging kitten with narrowed eyes.

"Aren't you interesting? Are you with him?" She looked between them, lips pursed. "My mistress will want to meet you two. Now, manners." Her eyes fixed on Cleo's, and her tone took on a hypnotic quality. "You will not touch me again."

The kitten's pupils nearly drowned her bicolored eyes. She spat at the vampire but dropped to the ground and slunk into the corner.

"As for you..." With the tip of her boot, the woman flipped the stake into her hand and drove it through Mathias's shoulder.

White-hot pain engulfed him. He grappled with the stake, but his hands were so weak he could barely grasp it. What was it made from? Nothing had ever affected him like this.

The room brightened. He blinked glazed eyes and saw, over the woman's shoulder, the quilt covering the mirror slip to the side.

The woman spun. "Stop, don't uncover it!"

But it was too late. Cleo gave a final tug on the blanket, and it fell away. Mathias's eyes widened. Instead of the woman's reflection, the mirror showed an enormous writhing creature made of smoke and fire. Compared to the one he'd seen earlier, it was a behemoth.

"The Mirror of Balance." Her voice was tinged with awe.

"It's true then. It shows your real form." She took a step toward it, then another. "No wonder she warned me not to look into it. She didn't want me to know I could defeat her."

In slow motion, the vampire knelt before the mirror. She stretched out a hand and caressed the image. The power spiked to a crescendo. Tendrils of light shot from the glass and speared the woman and Mathias. He jerked, fighting to pull away, but the energy combined with his weakness to hold him in place.

A strange, vibrating warmth crept through his veins. It drove away the lethargy in his muscles, permitting him to sit up. In front of him, tremors ran through the woman's body. She eased onto her side, like a leaf drifting to the ground.

Whatever was happening, Mathias wasn't about to waste the opportunity. He yanked the stake from his shoulder and leaped toward her. With as much force as he could muster, he drove the sharp wood deep into her back between the shoulders. The cords of light snapped back into the mirror with an audible pop.

She never made a sound. Her body crumbled to ash, releasing a cloud of smoke that flew into the glass. The mirror fell forward onto the vampire's remains, triggering a puff of dust. The energy in the room winked out.

Mathias sat back, stunned. What had just happened? Michelle's words from earlier floated back to him—weak becomes strong. The vampire had called it the Mirror of Balance. It had balanced their confrontation all right. He shuddered and scooted backward. If he'd been the stronger one in the room, he'd be nothing but a cloud in the mirror.

Something soft touched his hand. He glanced down, then swept Cleo into his arms.

"You did good," he whispered into her fur. Her small body vibrated with purrs. "Let's not hang around that thing, eh?"

Cleo squirmed from his arms and scampered out the door. Clearly, she agreed. Movement from the front room jolted him into the present. Erin and Michelle. He stumbled to his feet, cursing, and dashed after the kitten.

Erin was crouched next to Michelle, helping her sit up. "Matt!" Erin's voice was shaky. "What happened? Where's the psycho chick?"

"She's gone." Mathias ran a hand through his hair, dislodging some drywall dust. At least, he hoped it was drywall and not ash. He swallowed hard. "Are you both okay?"

"I... think so." Michelle wobbled to her feet. She looked at Mathias, and her hand flew to her mouth. "Your shoulder. You're hurt."

Mathias glanced down. His shirt was torn and bloody where she'd stabbed him, but he could feel the wound closing already. "It's not bad. We made a mess of your kitchen, though."

"I don't care about the dang kitchen." Michelle examined his shoulder, then threw her arms around him. She was trembling. "I'm so glad you're okay."

He patted her awkwardly, then extricated himself and stepped back. Michelle's cheeks flushed, and her shoulders slumped. His chest ached, but he shoved his feelings down. This evening was another reminder that she didn't belong in his world.

Erin's gaze shifted between them, and she pointedly changed the subject. "We need to call the police."

"Yeah." Michelle rubbed her arms, surveying the damage. "Why would she break into my house?"

"Did you see her eyes?" Erin shivered. "She must have been on drugs."

"No, she was after your mirror." Mathias fixed Michelle with a firm stare. "I didn't understand a lot of what she said, but it sounds like other people might come after it."

Michelle snorted. "What, like the antique mafia or something? That doesn't make sense."

"People don't make sense." He pulled out his cellphone. "Let the police take it into evidence until they can get to the bottom of it." The idea of that thing anywhere near her tied his stomach in knots.

"It's a family heirloom." Michelle's expression took on a stubborn cast. "If they break it—"

"I think Matt's right, Shelly."

Mathias blinked. He hadn't expected Erin to support him.

Erin scooped Cleo into her arms and stroked the kitten's chin. "Cleo hates it. I know that sounds like a dumb reason, but animals can sense dangerous chemicals. A lot of old mirrors contain mercury. Even if people weren't trying to steal it, I think you should store it somewhere until you get it tested."

Michelle screwed her mouth into a pout, but she nodded. "Fine. Is that what you think I should do, Cleo?"

Cleo licked her nose, nodded her head, and meowed. "Mmmyeah."

NIGHT MEWS

BY A.E. SANTANA

"Mreeeoow. Brrmreeoow."

I opened my eyes. Darkness swallowed the bedroom, as if I hadn't opened my eyes, as if I was still dreaming of being in the empty space before birth.

"Breeoow. Mreow."

Mau. I reached out my hand and felt her soft, furry head bump against my fingertips. My tired eyes darted over to the alarm clock on Whitney's side of the bed. It bled 3:45 p.m. Although I couldn't see my fiancé in the darkness, I worried Mau had woken her. But Whitney didn't move; she had learned to block out the cat's twilight romps. It was only Mau and I any time between one o'clock and four.

Although I grew up in the house we lived in—sold to us from my parents four years ago when they moved from the farm to the city—and although I knew every nook and creaking noise, the inky blackness blanketing the house at night unnerved me. I gritted my teeth, willing myself back to sleep.

Mau pushed the dome of her head against my fingertips, then grazed her cheek and mouth against them. The sides of her sharp teeth brushed against my skin. She wanted me to get up.

I hadn't had a full night's sleep since adopting Mau, a brown tabby kitten abandoned in a field near my parents' farm, seven years ago. From the first night in my old apartment nestled in the downtown area, it was screaming mews: adamant, needy, and hungry. From the first night, love and tenderness overwhelmed my heart, flooding my body with a turbulent joy.

In the beginning, Whitney had slept through Mau's hungry, ear-splitting mews. But me, a new mom for this tiny creature, had slept light, jumping up at every stir, every whimper—a sentinel's worry for this life I was in charge of—to feed or soothe.

That's how I felt about all my pets. Fierce, viciously protective, my happiness hinging on their well-being. I often remembered Sandwich and Sunshine, my childhood dogs I'd loved with an intensity that made me fight a rattlesnake to protect them in the old barn. Or the big orange cat, Jimmy, who wanted revenge on all humans for some unknown crime, who I won over with my steadfast devotion. There was always a cat or dog or rabbit or some animal that I protected, and they protected me.

You don't need protection, my parents had said, *why are you like this? So*—strung-out? Or they'd say, *animals don't know what they're doing. They're just animals.*

"Merreow."

Yes, Mau, I'm getting up.

As Mau grew from a tiny kitten into an incorrigible cat, her teeny mews became rumbling purrs, twittering meows, and nightly caterwauling. By the time we moved from the apartment to my parents' house, Whitney didn't always sleep through the night either. Mau had taken to pawing at our faces and galloping across the bed, playful during the recess of night, screaming into the darkness.

Yet, unlike in the apartment, I couldn't muster a smile or shrug off my cat's very cat behavior. In the darkness of the house, Mau's cries seemed to break through the logical barrier in my brain that told me there was nothing hiding in the shadows. Childhood fears of *something* otherworldly seemed not so childish while Mau roamed the house, wailing. There, her caterwauling was more like forlorn, guttural yeows than her excited mews and chirps. It was as if Mau was peering into the darkness and saying, "Mother, here it is, the thing that is keeping me up."

"Berreow."

I slipped out of bed and followed Mau, tiptoeing behind her like a frightened child. My eyes wide and heart beating furiously, I clutched my hands to my chest, afraid that something might take hold of them. What is it, Mau? What do you see? Will *I* see it? I don't want to see it. Also—There's nothing there. You're being dramatic. Silly. Neurotic: my parents' word.

"Mrrreeoow."

Mau and I stood in the small hallway. Two feet long at the most, long enough to hide whatever might be slinking in the dining room ahead of us or in the bathroom behind us. Long enough to become a home for unknown entities. I couldn't see Mau, but her tail flicked the tips of my toes, a small yet real comfort.

Mau, my sweet little girl, who napped with me in the morning or afternoons. She, who waited for me by the window whenever I came home. She, who made me laugh with her antics and made me feel special by sitting next to me, slow blinking at me, or resting a paw on my arm.

Mau stepped forward.

"Mreow. Mep. Brreow." Mother, around the corner. The thing. It is there!

Fear clawed its way into my mind. Too dark in the house. There's something in the dark!

You're just being uppity, I heard my parents echo in my head, *Relax.*

How could I relax? I wasn't about to let Mau deal with this *thing*—whatever it may be—by herself.

I trailed Mau, guided by my sense of where she was headed. I gulped down bile tracing acid along my throat. I hated going into the dining room in the dark. My grandmother's enormous, oval mirror sat on the wall in that room. It overlooked the weathered oak table with a gleam and glare weighted in secrecy and subtle malevolence.

That mirror had haunted my childhood. No one believed me, but even when fully dark, I could see a clear reflection in the mirror. The ability to see such a bright reflection in an otherwise black room caused havoc in my brain. *Restless,* my parents had called me. *Troubled,* they'd whispered.

When Whitney and I bought the house from my parents, I wanted to take the mirror down. But because the mirror was so heavy, it had been mounted in a way that fixed it to the wall and resisted our initial efforts to remove it. Too much effort, and Whitney wanted to ponder another solution; so, I'd draped a cloth over it, and that's how it stayed.

"Merreow."

Despair, a rotting pit in the center of my belly, throbbed within me. "Mau," I said, a gentle whisper falling out of my mouth like a dead leaf from a branch.

She responded with an array of tittering mews, acknowledging the attention she wanted from me.

You're not frightened, I thought. If you're not scared, then there's nothing to fear. "You would tell me, right?" I asked

Mau while she rubbed against my leg. "You'd hiss or run away, if there was something there, right?"

My parents had often told me I was too (neurotic, anxious) tenderhearted, that I was lucky that the farm I grew up on was no longer the working farm my mother had grown up on, and the only animals I knew there were pets. It had felt like my parents were shaming me.

They obviously didn't know the joys of loving an animal like family. They obviously didn't feel what I'd felt in the house at night, and how the nearness of those animals dispersed the unease of a lonely child. They also didn't understand how the animals kept finding me at the farm: Sandwich and Sunshine; Jimmy; Loopy, the brown rabbit who let me pick her up; and even Mau, who I'd rescued so close to my parents' property.

Little Mau. So earnest and affectionate, who trusted me enough to hand feed her and give coveted belly rubs.

"Meerp. Mreow."

In the darkness of the hallway, Mau's warm body against my leg left me feeling cold and helpless. She's not in danger, I told myself, *we're* not in danger. But it was the thought that maybe—possibly, somehow—Mau might be caught up in a dangerous situation that pushed me to follow her into the dining room, ignoring the way fear curdled inside me, making my skin crawl like an unwanted kiss.

The telltale thumps of Mau jumping on to the oak table echoed in the dark room. Whitney would have immediately shooed Mau down, but I let her. She was the one who knew what she was doing. I also didn't want to make any excessive movements or noises; I wanted to become one with the shadows. Please don't hurt me, I'm one of you.

"Brryeeeooooow! Yeeaauul!"

"What is it?" I whispered, although Mau was loud enough for us both. "What do you want?" I moved around the table, away from the shrouded mirror, toward the kitchen. "Snacks? Wet food?" Sometimes it was that. Some snacks or a spoonful of wet food would satisfy Mau and she'd nap until early morning.

"Yeeaaul! Brrreeeyeeooow!"

I steeled myself. "What is it, baby?" I asked. The darkness seemed alive around me, as if the *thing* Mau sensed would grab me—or her—at any moment. My heart sped up. No, I wouldn't let that happen.

"Brreeyeeaauul!"

She was looking at the mirror. Screaming at it. I couldn't see her, but I knew it. Knew, like I knew there was something wicked about the darkness of the house. Like I knew Mau was my baby—not just a cat, not just a pet.

"Let's go," I said, my voice sharper and louder than intended, fear taking hold of my vocal cords. "Mau, let's get into the kitchen. It's treat time!"

"Yeow! Brreemeow!"

I heard Mau tread across the table toward the mirror. That large glass and wrought iron monstrosity that seemed to creep around the edges of my memories, sending tendrils of terror into my already apprehensive childhood.

"Reeeooooyeeow!" Mother! It is here!

Desire to protect Mau broke through my fear, and I moved to scoop her up and run away back into the imagined safety of the bedroom. I reached out, stepped forward, leaning toward the area I thought she was, when the cloth on the mirror dropped.

"Rrreeooyeow. Yeeaauul."

The large oval mirror reflected the dining room. Mau stood at the edge of the table, glaring into the glass, and I stood at her side, shock enveloping my features. How can I see the room so clearly in the mirror when I can't even see in front of me?

Childhood terror devoured my frail adult cynicism. It's not possible, yet it's happening anyway, and I don't know what to do.

"Get away," I mouthed to Mau, no sound coming out. I swallowed, and my throat ached from dryness. "Get away," I said, licking my lips to bring moisture back to my mouth. "Mau, come here."

"Brroooyeow."

Movement in my peripheral vision. Something was *moving* in the reflection.

No, don't look. Not real. I'm being (neurotic) silly. Just a stupid mirror.

My lungs and ribs clenched, squeezing my heart. There's nothing there, I told myself. It's my reflection.

But I'm not moving.

Dread had grounded me again, my body tight like I was wearing an invisible straight jacket. What's happening?

Mau ignored my frozen panic. "Merreow," she said, "merp mep yeow."

"Come away," I tried to say. "Mau, come here. Let's go!"

"Meereow!"

My eyes, the only part of me that could move, shifted, and my heart stopped. The rigidity in my body swam away and a new sensation pulled me down, down, down.

Thinking back, it's difficult to place the feeling that chilled inside of me. Was it sadness? Was it bleakness? The closest emotion is hope; a terrible, ugly hope tainted with grief and the tormenting idea that maybe wishes do come true.

Instead of the reflection of the dining room, in the mirror were Sandwich and Sunshine. My two beautiful collie mixes my parents called annoying mutts, whom I loved with a harshness that burnt me inside out when they passed away. First Sunshine by getting hit by a car, then Sandwich two years later by some disease my parents hadn't vaccinated him against.

"Puppies?" I asked, the voice caught in my throat small and childlike. Tears stung my eyes. I didn't dare blink in case the vision of my beloved dogs vanished, along with the sick hope in my heart. My Sunshine and Sandwich back again. Chest heavy with love and sorrow, I glided toward the mirror I had feared my entire life, a moth to a flame. A mother to her children.

The image in the mirror sharpened, and the dogs were in a grassy meadow. Behind them, an orange blur sauntered up. Oh, my beautiful, grumpy tom cat, Jimmy, who'd scowled at me but allowed me to gently scratch behind his ears. My big, bad kitty who patrolled the farm and made me feel safe at night.

The tears came, a loosening of the forever-mourning from losing them. Sunshine and Sandwich and Jimmy—and there was Loopy, my field bunny; and the three unnamed kittens my parents didn't let me keep, but I loved anyway; and Bells, the stray dog I fed for two weeks before someone called the pound on him.

Standing at the mirror, my sorrow burned with regret and shame. "I couldn't save you," I said, the words cracked with the pain of a lonesome and fearful child who had too much love to give. Intelligently, I knew it wasn't my fault. Even though I called them my children, I was still a child. My parents were the ones who were in charge. It was up to Mom and Dad if the pet food was bought, if the pets were taken to the vet, if they were able to come inside the house, if they were even allowed to stay on the property. But I couldn't shake the shame of having not done enough. I was the one who loved them and that made them my responsibility.

Face wet and throat tight and dry, I reached out to the mirror. Sandwich, Sunshine, Jimmy, Loopy, Bells...

They're just animals, my parents had said. *Just animals.*

"No," I whispered, tears seeping down my chin and neck, dampening the collar of my pajama shirt.

How can I get in there? The thought approached me with a bluntness I wasn't ready for. Get into the mirror. The sturdiness of that thought left no room for doubt or fear.

We could all be together again. Brightness whirled inside of me; this was another chance to be a good mother. I hadn't had the power or knowledge to take care of them before. My heart sped up. As an adult, I could do better. Better than what I was able to do as a child, than what my parents had given them.

The despair I carried around after their deaths or disappearances seemed ready to melt away once reunited with them. Maybe the mirror was a passageway to heaven, a gateway to the afterlife. Maybe that's why I felt so weird around it.

Will I die? Will my soul leave my body and go into the mirror, or will my whole body go? Did it matter?

What about Whitney? But that thought was faraway and dim. Whitney was an adult human; she could take care of herself.

And Mau?

That stopped me. I tore my eyes away from the mirror and stared into the darkness Mau sat in.

"Baby?" I called out to her.

Can I take Mau with me? To the afterlife?

No, that would be the same as killing her. What would happen to Mau if I left her? Whitney might feed Mau, keep her water fountain clean, give her pets—but Whitney would not love Mau like I did. I didn't believe that Whitney would notice right away if something was wrong with Mau. She wouldn't choose to do a surgery or an expensive treatment to keep Mau alive and healthy if something unfortunate happened. Could I leave my baby to an unknown fate?

I turned back to the mirror, to my pets. My entire body

ached with the want of touching them, holding them, kissing them. How could I pass up this chance to be with them again? How could I invite the pain and grief of being without them back into my life?

Desire to crawl into the mirror and leave everything behind flooded me. Whitney and my parents and everyone else would get along fine without me. But I couldn't leave Mau.

"What do we do?" I asked Mau, while staring into the mirror. The dogs and the cats and rabbits and other animals all stared back. They must live in harmony in the afterlife, I thought. I can be there with them too.

"Grrreeeyeeaauul."

The noise was low, heavy, feral almost. I flinched at the sound of it. I shifted to face Mau in the darkness. Mau, why are you growling? This mirror turned out to be a good thing.

"Grrrrrrrrreeeeeeeeaaauul."

My confusion swirled into irritation. "Why now?" I asked Mau. "You didn't growl or hiss once at this mirror for four years, so why are you acting like this all of a sudden?" Tears bit into my eyes. Why do you have to be against the blessing of having my other babies back?

"You were the one who carried on all night about it!" My voice rose with each line. "And now you're growling?"

"Rrrrreeooowl!"

Crushed under hope and confusion and shame, I pressed a hand to my aching chest. Mau, don't do this to me.

They're just animals, my parents had said. Animals don't know what they're doing.

They do, I had retaliated. My parents were so sure that animals were dumb beasts, acting on instincts. I knew better, though. My pets knew they loved me. They knew they were protecting me, and they knew I loved and protected them.

I let out a strangled breath. Mau knew what she was doing.

I'd miss my pets forever, yet if Mau was upset, then there

was something I wasn't seeing. More prominent and fierce than rage or hope was my dedication to Mau. I believed Mau, believed her in a way my parents never believed me.

The decision wasn't without pain. Turning back to the mirror, my heart broke all over again. I said my pets' names to myself, or called them little babies, allowing my want to be with them to wash over me. But why are they all staring at me like that? Aren't they happy to see me too?

Is it really them? I looked closer.

My pets stared at me with neutral faces. They had moved in the mirror, but once settled into their place, either sitting or lying down, they were still. No tail swishing or ear twitching, no happy dog faces, no lazy yawns from the cats. Panic crept up on me, their statue-like composure unnerving me and twisting my insides into a knot.

This isn't right.

"Are you not my babies?" I asked in a whisper.

They all stood in unison and turned their faces toward me. There were still no tail wags or other normal animal behavior. Maybe because they are spirits?

Uneasiness spread through my nervous system. All I ever wanted was a second chance to be a good mother to the animals staring emotionlessly at me from the mirror. I clenched my teeth. How can a heart keep breaking?

I felt impossibly tired, as if my limbs and head weighed too much. The non-reaction from the animals that were perfect, spitting images of my pets bothered me. I had made the decision to stay with Mau, yet the thought that these pets were imposters frightened and saddened me. I didn't know the rules of the situation. Maybe it was really them? What do I do with this mirror and the maybe-but-not-maybe pets on the other side?

A soft head butted my arm. Mau. A melancholy yet

calming realization melted into me. It can't make up for the past, but I have the chance to be a good mom to Mau.

"Merrgreeeooowwl."

Fear suddenly flooded me. What if Mau tried to get into the mirror?

I stared into my grandmother's mirror. Staring back were my beloved pets who had brought me joy, companionship, love, and security in my childhood. I thought of Mau and—

"Babies," I said, my voice wavering, weak from emotion. "If it's really you, I know you'll understand." My eyes grew hot and wet. "You know I love you s—" I gulped, swallowing my broken words. "Love you so much." My bottom lip trembled, and my breath hitched. I rushed out my last words, fearing I might collapse into sobs. "Thank you for being there for me. For loving me. I'm sorry that I couldn't do better when I had you, but please know that I love you with all my heart."

I grabbed Mau and ran into the kitchen, with her wiggling in my arms. I placed Mau on the counter and poured her a handful of snacks. Quickly, I searched the cabinet under the sink for a wrench I knew was in there. When I found it, I stormed back into the dining room while Mau was busy snacking.

Impulsive, my parents had called me. *Neurotic, eccentric, uptight, antsy.*

You don't understand, I had told them. And I never understood why they were never as preoccupied with my well-being as I was for my pets.

I sucked in a big breath and forced myself to stare into the mirror one last time. "I love you," I said, and swung the wrench, hitting the mirror in the lower right corner and shattering that portion of it.

It was as if a light had winked out, and the image of my pets in the grassy meadow flickered out of sight. I dropped the wrench to the floor; it crashed into the shards of broken glass below. I leaned against the oak table and let my tears of frustration and grief fall.

I heard Whitney stumble awake, most likely alerted by the noise.

In the dark, I stared in the direction of the mirror that I had detested and, for a moment, gave me a glimpse of something beautiful, even if it wasn't real. I sighed deeply.

"Meeeooooow?"

I moved to stop Mau from coming any closer to the shards of broken glass. I met her at the kitchen entryway and picked her up again.

Soft, warm, comforting. With Mau in my arms—her small body feeling so vulnerable, but her presence so reassuring—my racing heart and mind finally felt consoled. Mau, my little guardian. You mean more to me than I can ever describe.

When Whitney turned the lights on in the kitchen, I stood away from the shattered mirror, my face smothered in Mau's fur, murmuring, "I love you, and I promise to protect you."

THE WHISPER ONES
BY S. FAXON

Carole sprawled her arms out across her couch.

"I *just* sat down," she declared to the living room, empty of any other souls but her cat. The heavy metal music the neighbors blared from their speakers might've been fun when she was in her teens, but she was over it as a working mom of two in her forties.

"Maybe I can ignore it," she said to her cat, Rufus.

She felt the raging beat pounding in her heart and looked longingly at the big glass of chilled Chardonnay in her hands. "So much for my quiet evening at home."

Bringing her chilled glass to her forehead, Carole remembered what her eight-year-old son had said about their quarterback sized male neighbors this morning: "They're probably meth-heads."

Her husband Greg had laughed when she'd set her hands on her hips and asked her son where he learned such a thing. While her son had stuttered for an answer, Greg had given her a sideways look while her twelve-year-old told her not to be so lame.

"Yep, that's me." After taking a big gulp of wine, while the music thudded, she added, "Lame ol' monster mom. The boring one with the rules and the office job. Dad's the fun one who gets to work from home."

It felt so unfair that she had to work long hours dealing with and solving the problems of faceless clients, while Greg in his sales job could take off whenever he wanted with the boys, like he did tonight. The boys weren't going to be back from their movie until after ten, so that left Carole and Rufus alone for the evening.

From her position on the couch, she whispered, "It's okay though, because my peaceful evening is being ruined by my psycho, probably meth-head neighbors." She pounded the rest of her glass, then poured another from the bottle she'd left on the pink marble coffee table.

She watched the wine in her glass ripple from the sound waves coming from next door.

This is ridiculous, Carole thought. *I'll have to deal with the neighbors. Bet the boys would never believe that I can handle a bunch of meth-heads. Dad's the cool one, the brave one.* She blew a raspberry. "If only the boys knew who really removed that spider from the kitchen last week."

Rufus meowed. His bright yellow eyes gazed into her soul before his white booted feet carried him out from the living room and up the stairs.

The beating drums and the singing guitars continued to rock.

"Really, guys?" She stood from her lounger and took her glass with her up the stairs. She imagined peeking out her window and seeing the college-aged neighbors shooting up meth in the backyard.

Wait, is that how you take meth? Do you smoke it?

She shook her head as she reached the landing and turned into her room. In the dim light from the hall, Carole saw

Rufus already inside. He sat on his haunches, staring at the golden framed mirror hanging on her wall.

"Is it speaking to you too, Rufus?" She approached the mirror. "I swear I heard voices out of it one summer at Grandma's house." Carole stared at its oval shape, looking at the detailed leaves carved into the frame. The experience of hearing voices from the mirror that summer hadn't frightened her in the slightest.

They'd intrigued her.

Who wouldn't be fascinated by an enchanted mirror?

Well, her mother, for one.

Carole sighed. That was the last summer her mother had let her stay at her grandmother's home. And while her sweet grandma had denied that voices were coming from the mirror, she'd always winked or given her a knowing smile that made Carole feel validated. Her mother had felt differently though when Carole had brought home the tale and had verbally attacked her each and every time she'd brought it up, until Carol gave up.

Carole wiped a tear from her cheek.

Grandma always had a way to make everything feel special. Even me.

She sniffled and said, holding her glass up toward the mirror, "Thank you for gifting it to me, Grandma. I promise I'll keep it safe."

Rufus meowed.

"That's right, Rufus, we both will."

The mirror rattled against the wall from the pounding sound waves.

Carole extended her hand, touching the mirror's frame to steady it. Her reflection was half concealed in shadow as she made eye contact with her own black eyes. Though she knew she was looking at herself, she said to her grandmother, "I really wish you were here with me."

Her hand slipped off the mirror.

"Alright, Rufus." She flipped the switch in the hall, concealing the room in darkness. "Let's see what those boys next door are up to and if we need to call the cops."

With her wineglass in hand, she crawled onto her bed. Settling with her knees on her husband's pillow, Carole parted the green curtains above her headboard ever so slightly. The window looked down onto the neighbor's flat roof and back yard.

A light fog was settling in for the night over the small valley her home on the hill presided over. In the near distance, downtown's skyscrapers twinkled and glowed just beyond the curving streets of her neighborhood. There was a time when Carole and Greg would just be getting ready to roll out to the downtown scene of America's Finest City, but it had been *years* since she and Greg had so much as gone on a date downtown, let alone clubbing.

And now I get my kicks spying on the neighbors. God, I'm becoming that nosey old lady every neighborhood has. Never imagined that for myself when I was growing up.

She patted the side of her thigh, inviting Rufus to join her. He jumped up on the window's sill, seemingly undeterred by the noise streaming up from next door. He released a long, gurgled meow as if reporting for duty. Carole rubbed his white-furred chin and then scanned every inch of the neighbor's yard. A few mismatched, rusting chairs sat empty in the weed-ridden yard. A lone warm white porch light shone out onto the concrete patio. Other than a couple of crumpled beer cans spilling out from an overfilled trash can, there was little else to see.

"It's so loud," she said to Rufus. He wasn't looking at her, though. His gaze was pointed back toward the mirror. "Maybe I really should call the cops."

"I wouldn't recommend that."

Carole spun around.

A woman stood in her doorway.

"Jesus!" Carole threw her glass at the stranger.

"Yo!" The stranger swung something in front of her.

Carole winced, waiting for the glass to shatter, but it never did. The glass fell harmlessly, weightlessly to the hardwood floor. Carole's jaw dropped. "Who are you? What're you doing in my house?" Carole's voice started out strong but withered down to a squeak.

How did the glass do that?

"Sorry," the stranger apologized. "I bungled this. Let me start over." A light illuminated out from the thing the stranger held.

Carole focused on the object. "Is that a... stick?"

"We'll get to that," the woman said. In the light, Carole realized this person wasn't a stranger. She was her neighbor from across the street.

Annie? No, shoot, that's her partner's name. Crap, what's her name?

Shaking her head, Carole held up her hand. "Again, why and *how* are you in my house?"

"Let's take a deep breath," the neighbor advised, breathing deep as if to show Carole how. "I came in through the front door."

"But it was locked." Carole specifically remembered turning the deadbolt.

I always obsessively check the locks when I'm alone.

"Well," the neighbor started. "It was. But you called me over... *so* I'm a little confused as well."

How much wine did I drink?

"When did I call you over?"

Shrugging, the neighbor said, "I don't know... like two minutes ago?" She pointed to the mirror. "Could've been less. You finally used it, so I was, admittedly, overly excited."

Carole's jaw dropped. "Sorry, what?"

"The mirror?" She looked at Carole as if it, her entrance, and her glowing stick were the most normal thing in the world. "You know... your grandma's mirror. C'mon, stop joking around." She smiled as if this was an elaborate prank Carole was pulling.

But Carole was not laughing. She felt sweat forming around her hairline.

Rufus jumped down from the sill and crossed the bed to the neighbor. The neighbor bent over to stroke his chin, which Rufus accepted with a big cat grin.

"Ok, ok, back up," Carole started, but the neighbor's name flashed into her mind. "Maeve! Maeve, what about the mirror?"

Maeve's smile faded. "Wait, you're serious?"

Carole raised her brows. "Yeah, I'm literally and figuratively in the dark, so if you could *please* fill me in on who you really are or how the hell any of this is happening, that'd be *great.*"

"Again, I am *so* sorry," Maeve apologized, holding her hands up. She held the stick flat out, wedged between her thumb, palm, and pinky. "I really bungled this. Um, ok, well, I guess the best place to start is who I am."

Carole's nervous laugh confirmed her guess.

"Right, well..." Maeve scratched her black-dyed hairline. "My name really is Maeve. I really am your neighbor, and I knew your grandmother. She and I met through the society we both belong to."

Carole winced. "My grandmother is gone. She doesn't belong to anything anymore."

"I'm sorry, in our society, you're always a member. The society is how we kept safe, how we kept the world safe for a *very* long time."

"What is the society? And why is that important right

now?" Carole's memory flashed her through a dozen documentaries she'd recently binge-watched on Netflix. "Oh my God, is it like some sort of cult?"

Maeve held her hand over her heart as if the society was the most precious thing in the world to her. "It's not a cult, but throughout the centuries, our people have been known as many things; some quite negative, the least of which being witches." She paused as if to give Carole a moment to process that. "There are many today who call some of us, like myself, and your grandmother—Guardians—but all of us, all of our kind, like to think of ourselves as the whisper ones."

Carole's jaw dropped. Her widened eyes stared at the stick with the light glowing out from its end. "Witch? Like... Harry Potter? So is that an um..." Her whispered words were drowned out by the blaring music next door, but her pointed finger gave Maeve enough of an idea of what she said.

"This?" She held up the stick. "Yeah, it's a wand and while in many ways we are like that Wizarding World, in other ways we are different."

"Like being real?"

Maeve smiled. "Yeah, I guess that's a good one. Like them, because of persecutions from the non-enchanted, we've hid for centuries. Our society, The Guardians, was formed in the 1800s as an elite group to help maintain balance in this world over other enhanced ethnicities. Your grandmother and me and countless others, we're a part of that society. We're called Guardians because we keep the peace. Carole, your grandmother never told you *any* of this?"

Carole looked at the mirror. Her heart raced. "I..." her voice cracked as emotions overwhelmed her. "She always said the mirror would be here for me, but I thought literally, not in this mental-breakdown-esk way." She ran her hands over her face and exhaled sharply. "Wait, so back up... like whisper ones, are... am *I* a whisper one? What does that mean?"

Maeve nodded. "We pass through the streets like moths in the night. Being a whisper one is typically passed down from parents to their children. The powers within you are taught, as much as inherited. I don't know the full story, but I think your mom wanted nothing to do with it, so..." She shrugged. "It'd make sense that she didn't teach you and why you're in the dark."

Carole ground her teeth. She scooted off the bed and looked at Rufus. He stared at her as if he was completely up to speed and waiting for her to catch up. Between the music next door and this ludicrous lapse in a coherent state, Carole was done. "Ok. This is a nervous breakdown. I saw that professor have it that time in college, but I think he was high on something, maybe that's it. Maybe my crazy meth-head neighbors somehow are pumping meth up and out into the air and now I'm dealing with the repercussions of their vapors."

"That's really not how that..."

"Shut up."

"Ok." Maeve sucked her lips in.

Carole stared into Maeve's eyes. The woman looked at her with care and concern, not what Carole would have expected from someone telling her anything like this, which made it worse. "Ok, I really can't..." Carole held her fist to her forehead. "I can't right now. I have to go call 9-1-1 to tell them that the neighbors are endangering me with their meth vapors, and they'll get arrested, and tomorrow, if I'm not in a straitjacket, I'll come over, and we'll talk this out. Ok? Ok, bye."

Carole started to push Maeve toward the door, but her unexpected and unwelcome guest rotated so that their stances switched. "I wouldn't call the cops." Maeve advised.

Carole's expression dropped. "Of course. Why?"

Maeve took a delicate step toward her. "If you didn't believe the first part, you're sure not going to believe anymore." Carole's expression remained unchanged. "You know what?" Maeve bit her lip. "I'll just go deal with them. Please don't call the police."

Maeve walked past Carole and headed down the stairs.

For a second, Carole felt the weight of a bus roll off her shoulders, until she made eye contact with Rufus.

Wait...

Carole ran after Maeve down the stairs and caught her right before she reached for the closed and locked front door. "Maeve, what the heck are you going to do with the guys next door? Just one of them is three times your size."

Maeve chuckled. "I told you, I'm a peacekeeper. This is my job; keeping stupid asses like them from exposing our community."

Once more, Carole's jaw dropped. "Are they..." she gulped. "Whisper ones too?"

Shaking her head, Maeve said, "No."

"Well, what are they, then? What else is a part of this 'community'?" Carole used dramatic air quotes around the last word.

Maeve set one of her hands on Carole's shoulder as if to steady her. "You sure you want to know?"

Carole narrowed her gaze. "Try me."

Maeve leaned closer and whispered, "Werewolves." She leaned away and saw Carole's brows raise. "They're werewolves. Our community is composed of three ethnic groups—werewolves, whisper ones, and vampires."

That's it.

"Get out of my house," Carole demanded in a growl. "Or I will call the cops on *you*."

Maeve smiled. "Give me five minutes, and I'll get the sound turned down, ok? The next door stuff is a walk in the park. It's *you* I'm worried about. I just dumped a mountain of fantasy on your head, and you probably haven't even had dinner yet."

"Get out." Carole reached for the door, but with a flick of the stick in Maeve's hand, the deadbolt and the round handle lock turned without being touched. The door then opened with an invisible hand.

Carole shot her gaze to Maeve's.

Maeve winked at her and said, "After I get the guys quiet next door, get some rest, Carole. I'll be back tomorrow. We'll talk then."

———

Get rest, Carole, Carole thought angrily to herself after shutting the door behind Maeve. *Go back to your lame life, Carole. I'm a five-foot-two woman who looks like I should be an eccentric schoolteacher, but I'm going to go tell those* werewolf *boys what's what.*

"God, what is happening right now?" Carole stormed off to the living room, her bare feet slapping against the wooden floor. She snatched the wine bottle from the table, put it to her lips, and threw it back. As she chugged down what felt like a glass full, she saw Rufus in the corner of her eye. He was sitting on the stairway, staring at her.

"What?" she asked him, waving the wine bottle. "Are you going to start talking to me like you're Thackery Binx?"

The cat flattened his expression.

Carole gulped.

"You... *do* understand me, don't you?"

Rufus blinked, then leaned far over to the side to awkwardly lick his shoulder.

"Ok, maybe you're still just a cat. A smart cat, but not a mythical, supernatural being."

Carole's knees bent, dropping her to the couch.

"Ok." She held her hands out in front of her. "Let's assume you're not hallucinating, Carole. Let's be open to this.

Magic is real." She breathed in slowly. "My grandma was a witch. A real freaking witch, and she belonged to a secret policing society... that's kinda awesome." She looked at Rufus. "Right?"

He meowed and then continued to groom himself.

"Right." She leaned back into the embrace of the couch. The music next door was still thumping. Pulling the bottle of wine back to her lips, she checked her watch as she drank. "It's been like three minutes. What if she's not as capable as she thinks she is?" She set the bottle flat against her stomach and chest. "Werewolves. I'm stuck on werewolves. Like magic, ok, I see that, but freaking werewolves? That's gotta be a joke or a metaphor for something else."

Rufus ran down from the stairs and ran over to her. He jumped up on her lap, setting his forepaws on her chest over the sides of the bottle. His nose was less than a hand's distance from her own. Carole scratched the back of his head. "Is this your way of telling me to get off my butt and go see for myself?"

He purred.

"Or are you just demanding to be petted? I see how it—"

The music stopped.

Carole popped up from the couch, sweeping Rufus from her chest and down to the couch. After barely catching the bottle, she set the wine on top of the table as the silence surrounded her. "She did it, she—"

A great crash echoed from next door.

"Maeve!"

Carole ran to the back door. She rushed out into the night, slamming the door behind her, sealing Rufus inside. Her hand reached out, grabbing the broom from beside the door as she ran toward the short fence between the two houses. She stepped up on her cinder block garden, leaping over the wooden fence into the neighbor's yard.

Her rational mind knew better than to storm the door, and what on earth could she really do with a broom, but her pounding heart knew she had to be there, that she had to try something.

Clutching the broom in her quaking hands, Carole approached the green back door. The black window screen hung loosely down, reflecting the care the owners of the house had given it, all of these years. Carole breathed slowly through her mouth. *Do the owners know their renters are wolves? Are they actually wolves themselves? Ok, wait. Focus, how can you—*

The door swung open.

Carole jumped back, holding the broom's stick in front of her like a sword.

One of the neighbor boys with blond hair stared at her.

From somewhere deep inside, Carole felt a tingling power growing. Her grip on the broom tightened, her stance shifted forward. It felt as if a warrior within her was awakening.

"Where's Maeve?" she asked, her voice steady.

The young man crossed his arms over his thick, built chest. "Who?"

Carole flexed her grip on the broom. "Our neighbor across the street. I know she's here. Where is she? Is she ok?"

He ran his blue eyes all over her, checking her aggressive stance. "Um, you're trespassing. Not sure I should tell you anything."

"Stop messing around," Carole's heart beat like a drum, summoning within her more courage than she knew she had within her. "Maeve came over, the music stopped, and then I heard a bang. I'll ask again, where is Maeve?"

"Hey, Ryan!" another male's voice called from inside.

The man talking with her looked over his shoulder into the dark room. Carole tried to alter her view around the man, trying to see what she could of the inside, but only a low blue light glowed in the far background.

The voice said, "Stop being a jerk. It's ok, let her in."

Ryan opened his arms and said, "No way, man, she—"

"Let her in." Maeve's voice demanded. "If you want my help, let her in."

Ryan turned back to Carole. He glared at her another minute, then opened the door fully.

Carole flexed her grip on the broom once more but took slow steps forward. Ryan didn't budge from his spot, letting her pass by him. Heat radiated from his body as she brushed against him. He whispered, "Tell anyone what you see here..."

Carole flashed a quick smile though sweat gathered on her hairline. *I'm in the house of either werewolves or meth-heads. And one of them just threatened me. So not how I envisioned this night going at all.*

She continued to hold on to the broom, keeping it tight as if it was a talisman helping to keep her bravery true.

"We're back here, Carole," Maeve instructed, her voice coming out from what Carole assumed to be a bedroom.

Though the house was dim, she could make out the living room, sparsely furnished with lumpy, secondhand chairs and a coffee table. For a house of frat boys, it was surprisingly clean. There were no blatant drug paraphernalia or smutty photos scattered about, as she and her husband had often imagined and joked about. Her paced, barefooted steps led her to the room where Maeve's voice had come through.

The blue light glowed. It took Carole's eyes a moment to adjust, but what she saw stole her breath.

Sprawled out on a mattress on the floor was a larger-than-life man, or at least his shape was that of a bodybuilder, but his elongated snout and ashen colored fur brought the word rocketing into Carole's mind.

Wolf. He's a freaking werewolf.

Carole's jaw dropped.

On one side of him was another of her neighbors and on

the other was Maeve. The glowing blue light emanated from the tip of her wand. Maeve ran it in slow, sweeping motions over the werewolf's body, her eyes shut softly as if contentedly lost in a meditative trance.

Ryan came up behind Carole, standing in the hall.

The other neighbor on the floor, Ron, she thought his name was, had his hands folded as if in prayer up to his chin. His wide eyes watched their wolf companion's chest rise rapidly up and down.

"What's happening to him?" Carole whispered.

Ryan leaned close and said, "He's bugging out."

Carole raised her shoulder and said, "I don't understand."

Ryan sighed, still clearly irritated by her presence. He explained, "It means he's stuck in this form. He's been going back and forth between wolf and man, half transformed, for hours. He came to us because we're his brothers. The music was to help cover up the sound of his screams."

"Screams?" Carol asked, transfixed by the calming blue hues flowing from Maeve's wand.

"Yeah," he snorted. "Think it's easy going back and forth between wolf and man? It sucks."

"You're lucky I came when I did," Maeve said, her eyes still in that meditative state. "If I hadn't knocked him out with that sedation spell, his heart might've stopped. Why didn't you call your alpha?"

Even though Ryan was behind her, Carole swore she could feel him shrinking inside.

Maeve shook her head, her hand never wavering from its task. "Next time, call your alpha. He's a good man."

Carole continued to watch the wand. Its pendulum movements were so soothing. Time slipped away until finally, the werewolf's breathing regulated, his flexed, furred, and clawed hands relaxed.

Carole gasped and covered her mouth as the fur and snout

retracted. Carole cringed. His bones snapped, and muscles twitched as his form transitioned from wolf to man.

A collective sigh of relief filled the room as the handsome, bare form of her neighbor replaced the wolf. Carole shot her eyes away from his nudity. *Last thing I need is for my husband to find out about this. About any of this.*

Maeve gave the brothers instructions on how to care for their exhausted fellow, how to contact their alpha, and how she was right across the street should anything like this happen again.

"For now, just let him sleep," Maeve finished. She looked at Carole, and with a flick of her head, motioned it was time for them to leave.

Carole nodded and said her goodnights to the boys, who, she realized, weren't too unlike her sons. Especially as they were indeed not meth-heads.

———

Stepping out into the cool night, Carole took a moment to look up at the stars. Though they were on the edge of the city and the map of the heavens was mostly lost to her eyes, she swore she saw a star shoot across the sky.

"You'll start to see things a bit different from now on," Maeve said as the pair of them slowly walked from their neighbor's front porch toward Carole's home. "You've sure been thrown into the deep end tonight."

You could say that again.

Framed in the window of her front room, Rufus stared out at them standing in the driveway.

Carole chuckled. "To think, magic was in the mirror all of this time."

Maeve scratched her neck. "Well, kind of. Think of the mirror as a pager; they're how we've communicated for a very long time. The true magic," she tapped Carole's chest. "Is in there. But it's up to you if you want to... you know, join the club." She winked. "We do some pretty cool stuff."

"A whisper one?" Carole asked. "I can... become one?"

"You *are* one," Maeve insisted. "You just have to learn how to embrace and use what's always been inside you."

Carole bit her lip. Her eyes filled with tears. "How can I be? I've always played it so safe. My kids and my husband think I'm boring."

Holding up her shoulders, Maeve said, "I think you proved otherwise tonight. You literally came to a house full of werewolves tonight barefoot with a broom. That doesn't sound like something a boring person would do."

"Just a dumb one," Carole joked. She pointed at the broom she still held. "Seriously? Even if they weren't... werewolves, what could I have done?"

Maeve flicked the broom's handle and said, "You're a witch; you coulda taken flight."

Carole's eyes doubled. *Holy... is that real?*

Maeve laughed. "Go on inside, and get some rest, Carole. There's no need to sign up for this membership right away. The offer will always be here for you." Maeve rubbed Carole's arm and walked away.

Carole looked back up to the stars. She thought of the mirror in her room and all the magic that had surrounded it. Not merely that of the whisper ones, but of her grandmother. Of all the happiness and care and love that woman had always given her, no matter what. Carole missed her with all of her heart. And while she'd thought the hole in her heart would never mend, the love they shared had never left.

To the heavens she said, "Now I know how I can honor you in the way you always honored me." Turning to Maeve, she said, "Hey!"

Halfway across the street, Maeve turned around on her

heels. The raised-browed look on her face showed her excited anticipation of being called back.

The smile on Carole's face said it all, but she held up two thumbs and said, "I'm in. See you tomorrow?"

Maeve nodded. "Sounds like a plan."

***

The front door opened.

Carole remained on the couch, a half-eaten bowl of microwave popcorn beside her. *Friends* played on the T.V. and Rufus was stretched across her lap.

Her sons waved and yelled, "Hi, Mom," as they darted up to their bedrooms. Carole knew they'd whip out their Switches and play until they fell asleep. She'd go in there in about an hour's time to take off their headphones and tuck them into bed.

Without looking at him, she knew Greg had kicked off his shoes as he pulled out his wallet and keys from his pockets. The keys made the same clanking sound they did every time he placed them on the stand beside the door.

As he approached, the look he gave Carole was happy but concerned. "Hey," he started. "Sorry I didn't let you know about the movie earlier."

Carole brought popcorn into her mouth and shrugged. "It's ok. Turned out, I had a pretty interesting evening anyway."

Looking at the T.V. Greg sighed and said, "I see that. *Friends* again?"

She shrugged once more and said, "It's my comfort show."

"I know, I know." He contemplated her a moment before leaning in and kissing her. "Alright, well, I'm off to bed."

"Alright, well, love you."

"Love you."

Greg patted her leg before turning up the stairs. She knew he was going to bed; he'd scroll news for an hour and then pass out with his phone on his chest. On any other night before when this exact scene had played out, Carole might have cried, curled up and questioned every element of her life, but tonight, she smiled.

Rufus sat up on her lap. Scratching his chin, she whispered to him, "Let's keep what happened tonight just between us?" Rufus meowed. She chuckled, then added, "They don't need to know that *I'm* not the boring one."

Grandma Ruth's Legacy

Donna Marie West

My grandmother was a cat lover. No, that's not accurate. She was the crazy cat lady the neighbors talked about or avoided or occasionally brought their unwanted kitties to.

Grandma Ruth couldn't resist the battered stray tom, the sickly kitten, or the elderly house cat that had been left alone when its equally elderly human passed away. She took them all in, caring for them as if they were her babies—and I guess they were, as she often called the cats her "fur babies." She wasn't always that way, but once her only child—my dad—left for college, and after my grandfather passed away when I was just a toddler, the cats became everything for her. At one point, she must have had a dozen adults and a couple litters of kittens in the house, not to mention the handful of feral cats that came to eat the food she put in bowls in her backyard. Then the cancer she'd been fighting for years forced her to make contingency plans. She found homes for all but two of her indoor cats but knew she didn't have to worry about them. I'd promised to look after any that were left the day she told me she was dying.

Grandma Ruth had passed away ten days ago, leaving me her cottage on the edge of town and everything in it—furniture, appliances, dishes, and her remaining kitties—and enough money to keep us going for quite some time.

"Don't you worry, I'll take good care of you," I promise the indoor cats, as they watch me carry the last of my boxes into the house. I had come by every day to give them fresh food and water and clean out their litter box in the laundry room, but this is the first night I'm officially out of my parents' house for good. I put the box down in Grandma Ruth's—now my—bedroom and look at the black-and-white male who followed me and now sits, eyeing me from the bed.

"You're a good boy, Boxer," I croon. He'd been stretched out alongside my grandmother's body when the hospice nurse had come in to find her dead that morning.

I sit down beside him and run my hand through his short, thick fur. Despite having lost a front leg to infection when he was only a few months old, the middle-aged tripod cat is an active, healthy boy.

He leans against my hand and breaks into loud purrs.

A moment later, Gracie, a slate-gray female who is easily twenty years old, climbs with some effort onto the bed to join us.

"I know you miss her," I say to both over a sudden lump in my throat. "I miss her too."

Blinking back tears, I take Gracie into my arms and kiss the top of her head. I can feel all the bones in her warm little body through her thin coat. I know she's in the final stages of renal failure and despite the best of diet and veterinary care, she doesn't have much time left.

Gracie snuggles against me but isn't paying any attention. Her golden eyes are wide and unblinking as she stares at the big oval mirror hanging above the six-drawer walnut dresser.

I can see our reflection in the antique glass that's tarnished in the corners. The mirror has always held a fascination for me. When I was twelve years old, I spent two weeks of my summer vacation with my grandmother. I helped her repaint the wood frame with a gold colored-paint so that it looked gilded. While we worked, she had told me the story of the mirror.

"It was already an antique when my mother gave it to me as a gift on my thirty-first birthday. It had been passed down through her family for oh, five or six generations. Just like our red hair and freckles, it's our legacy, I guess you could say. One day, I'll pass it on to you.

"Anyway, Mother said she'd never told me before, although I'd suspected something, that the mirror is mystical. A window into another world, she'd said, and I would see for myself soon enough.

"Of course, I laughed and thanked her, but I didn't believe a word of it. Well, at least not at first. But I've seen things in it over the years, when I look at it out of the corner of my eye, or when I'm just drifting off or waking up. I've seen your grandfather, God rest his soul. And I've seen the most beautiful place," she had smiled, and her hazel eyes had lit up when she said this, *"a place where all the cats are happy and healthy and ready to love and be loved. That's the place I want to go when I die—where your Grandpa George and all the kitties I've lost over the years are waiting for me."*

I remember something else she'd said about the mirror only last year, when she knew her days were numbered:

"I think we see into the mirror more clearly and more often as a soul approaches the end of its earthly life. It doesn't have to be our own soul, though. Just someone we're close to. The kitties see

it too. I'm sure of it." And she had that smile again, like she knew something I didn't.

With Grandma Ruth's words echoing in my mind, I glance at the mirror every few minutes as I unpack my clothes and place them in the drawers and closet my brother Andy and I had emptied just two days ago. We'd taken her clothes and shoes to the local homeless shelter as she'd requested, but I'll go through her personal things—photograph albums and old letters, bric-à-brac and boxes up in the attic full of God only knew what—later, when I have the heart for it.

I have terrible trouble sleeping that first night. Truth be told, as sad as I am, being alone in my grandmother's house— in the bedroom where she slept for fifty-odd years and died, no less—creeps me out.

Then there's the mirror. I can't help looking at it every few minutes, noticing the gorgeous half-moon reflected in it.

When I look a bit later, the moon is gone.

That's weird, I muse remembering there was a waning moon in the evening sky just a few nights ago.

I snuggle closer to the kitties and finally drift off with Boxer purring in my ear and Gracie curled up against my thigh.

I'm worried about Gracie. Over the week since my arrival, her condition has visibly deteriorated. When she isn't sleeping on my bed or the armchair in the living room, she's in the litter box or drinking water from the bowl in the kitchen. She's still eating but had vomited the food back up several times, always looking up at me with those big, golden eyes and an expression that seemed to say, "I'm sorry," as I cleaned up the mess.

That Saturday afternoon, I find her sitting on my bed like a little sphinx, front legs stretched out in front of her, eyes fixed on the mirror as if she sees something more interesting than the reflected image of the spruce tree outside the window. I sit with her for a while, just stroking her soft fur and telling her she's a good kitty, and I love her, until I have to get up and get ready for company.

My parents and Andy are coming for supper and an evening of reminiscing about Grandma Ruth. I'm not sure if I'm looking forward to it, but we order Chinese food—all our favorite dishes—and the meal goes down easily enough, punctuated by somewhat bittersweet conversation. Dad was never really close to his mother, and I figure he's here more for Andy's sake and mine than his own. Mom probably talked him into it.

It seems I'm right because after supper, at my mom's insistence, Dad and Andy climb the narrow ladder to the attic and bring down a couple dusty cardboard boxes smelling of mothballs and holding what turns out to be the birthday, Christmas, and Easter cards Grandma Ruth received from friends and family ever since she was a little girl.

We spend several nostalgic hours sipping coffee and passing the cards between us until Dad holds one up to read aloud.

"My dearest Ruthie, I believe the time has come for you to have my mirror. It is a gift in more ways than one. A hundred years ago a woman with 'the sight' crafted it. It can give the viewer a peek into another realm—but whether it shows us where we will go when we die, I truly do not know. I hope it does. I offer it to you, hoping you will come to appreciate its gifts as I have. Perhaps you will understand them better than I do. Love, Mom."

Dad gingerly places the card down on the coffee table as if he's afraid to hold it any longer and gives me a sharp look. "Anna... please tell me you aren't planning to keep that cursed thing."

"I don't know yet," I reply. "It's still there in the bedroom. Why? Dad, did you ever see anything in it?"

He shakes his head. "No. I know Mom did, though she didn't talk to me about it much. I guess she didn't want her only child thinking she was batty. She did mention once seeing her parents and an older brother who was killed in World War Two. And one time, a beautiful garden in the sunrise, and something about a big half-moon."

A half-moon? I remember what I saw the other night. *No way! Could it have been...?*

I decide I'll keep the mirror even as Dad goes on, speaking in a low voice, half lost in his memories. "I had a dog, a border collie, back before Mom went all out on the cats—"

"Queenie," says Andy, interrupting. "You've told us about her before."

"Yes, well..." Dad clears his throat and reaches for his coffee cup, which is empty. He puts the cup down again and continues. "I'm sure she saw things in that mirror. She'd spend hours lying on the rug beside Mom's bed, just staring into the glass. God knows what she saw, but sometimes she'd be wagging her tail. Other times, she'd let out the most baleful howl I've ever heard. Mom said Queenie saw doggy heaven and later, she said her cats saw kitty heaven." He gives me a sad smile. "Speaking of cats... Andy says he saw a couple the other day?"

"Yeah, Grandma Ruth left me two—Boxer and Gracie. They're probably sleeping on the bed. Gracie's really old and sick. She doesn't have much time left." I sigh at the thought of burying her in Grandma Ruth's kitty cemetery out in the back field, but I'll do it, because my grandmother asked me to.

We look at the last of the cards. Dad and Andy put them all away sorted by year while Mom helps me with the supper dishes. They leave around midnight, and I'm alone again with the kitties who are, as I guessed, waiting for me in the bedroom.

Vacation and sick days all used up; I go back to work on Monday. I don't plan to live on my grandmother's money. When I'm home, I try to spend as much time with the cats as I can—especially Gracie, who has stopped eating and is growing weaker by the day.

I make an appointment with the veterinary clinic to take her on Thursday evening to be put to sleep. No point delaying the inevitable or letting her suffer needlessly.

Gracie, however, has other ideas. She's so active on Wednesday evening that I wonder if I should cancel tomorrow's appointment. She eats most of her supper and keeps it down, and even joins Boxer in playing with one of their multiple fluffy mouse toys. That night she actually jumps up onto the bed and falls asleep purring in the crook behind my knees.

I wake up as dawn is breaking. Boxer is sitting on the corner of the bed, ears perked and tail swishing slowly. He stares at Grandma Ruth's mirror, where the sun shines yellow in a pale blue sky above a garden full of rose bushes and lavender.

Am I still asleep and dreaming? I blink a couple of times and rub my eyes. Nope, I'm awake, and the scene is still there. This time, a petite woman with red hair, wearing a white summer dress, strolls through the grass between rows of rose bushes, a slate-gray cat frolicking at her sandaled feet. The woman stops and reaches down. The cat jumps right up into her arms and cuddles against her chest.

I push myself up in bed, gaping at the glass, realization dawning that the mirror truly is mystical. The scene slowly fades away to be replaced by the spruce tree outside the window, faintly lit by a normal, pink, and orange dawn sky.

And I know before I reach out to touch Gracie's cool, stiff form curled up near where my legs were before I sat up. Boxer turns to look at me with the saddest green eyes. He knows too.

Gracie has gone to join Grandma Ruth in their very own shared vision of heaven, and we've seen them on their way.

For Yours
By Chris Bannor

Friskies.

"What?"

I want Friskies.

"You're kidding, right?"

When have I ever?

Dany turned her head to the side. "Where the hell am I supposed to find a box of Friskies?" There was no answer, not the ghostly sound of Adam's voice in her head, nor a growl from behind her. The giant cat didn't respond to her question, but she didn't expect him to. He was already lying behind her, his dark gray head resting on his giant white paws. She could feel him falling asleep. At least they were safe for the night. The big cat looked like a gray tiger and had a sense of danger that far outstripped any of its native counterparts. "Alright," she said as she leaned against his side, taking comfort from his warmth. "We'll see what we can find."

It was the best she could offer. It wasn't like she could run to the nearest store and pick some up. Oh, how she missed the convenience of convenience stores.

The night was chilly, but with Adam at her back, her

jacket kept her warm enough. She let her head fall against the sleeping cat's back and stared up at the stars. There was no more light pollution, so the stars were much easier to see than they used to be. Maybe she should crawl through one of the crumbling stores and find a book about the constellations. It would be something interesting to do on the days when they were unable to travel.

The stars used to call to her, like a dream coming to take her away. Now they were closed, and she had no choice but to make her way on such crude ground, soil, grass, rock, and concrete as she could. Humanity's exodus to the stars had taken over fifty years, but the last of the shuttles had escaped Earth ten years ago.

The people left behind had to fend for themselves.

The day they had put Adam in her head was the day they'd doomed her to this planet. It was a day she both cursed and revered. She'd agreed to be a test subject on the bonding experiment to help pay her way off the planet. They were supposed to bond her to the modified animal for three months. Once they ran their tests and saw it was stable, they'd remove the bond and the animal's thoughts from her mind. Then she could go to the stars. The bond proved unbreakable though, as the other test subjects had learned the hard way. She became a Hack that day with the tech permanently fused to her brain, unable to leave for the colonies she'd spent a lifetime dreaming of.

Those able to go to the colonies blamed Mods and Hacks for the wars that had destroyed humanity and left the Earth a wasteland. Dany had learned in school the wars were fought over politics. But really, they were fought because humans enjoy being right more than they enjoy helping each other. On one side were the Mod soldiers with their obvious enhancements and the Hacks that drove the intelligence agencies. On the other side was everyone else. Eventually, the politicians gave up on saving what was left of humanity and talked about heading to the stars. But not with those that had caused the Earth's destruction. So, Mods and Hacks were prohibited from entering the spaceports. She and those like her were held accountable for the destruction wrought by the generation before her.

The same day that took away her chance to leave for the colonies had also given her Adam; a lifelong companion and her dearest friend. He was the last breed of genetically modified cats, big enough to be a true predator with stronger instincts, higher intelligence, and an implant in his head that allowed him to speak directly into her brain. Adam was both Mod and Hack, and Dany wouldn't have survived this world long without him.

The day she met Adam the scientists had successfully implanted four pairs of Hacks that day. The other three had their implants removed three months later. Dany had canceled the procedure and rescheduled because of the flu. It was the best luck in her life. All six who underwent the procedure, cats and humans, died as soon as the scientists cut the bond. Dany ran from the safe centers when she found out, though the scientists had promised her they'd learned from their mistakes, and the procedure would be safe now. She took Adam and anything she could and fled to find a new life in the abandoned cities. Adam had been no more willing to die than she had. They'd been guinea pigs enough.

Go to sleep, Adam grumbled, hearing her thoughts about the past. He purred softly though, and she smiled up at the stars. When she closed her eyes on the roof of the abandoned school, she trusted Adam to keep her safe.

Two days later, they were walking along the coastline. Adam didn't like the water, and he hated the sand, but there were usually traders along the coast, and they could use news. Traders were the best way to get rare items and were even better as a source of news, gossip, and rumors about the different territories. Dany didn't like using them. Nothing was free with them, but it was the only way to hear info about the larger roaming gangs that might rob her and stay informed on which settlements had survived and were still viable. The traders were Hacks like her, passing information to one another through a system implanted into the brain.

Today's trader was willing to share information for a few pieces of tech Dany had found a few weeks back. A better deal than she usually got, but his wagon was riding low to the ground, and it looked like his lifter that would let the wagon float over the rocks and debris was about to die. His shelves were bare, and what he had wasn't anything special. They all hit hard times now and then. She passed him the parts as Adam watched at her side.

"Where is the safest haven these days?" she asked.

"There's a place up north, to the east of the River," the trader said. "Been stable about six months now. People seem to like it well enough. The only name I hear them call it is Home."

"Stable after only six months? What's the catch?"

"Nothin' I've heard of," he said. "Everything seems to be on the up and up. Everyone who comes out of Home says they're treated well and fairly. No one's talking about who runs it or how it's run, though."

It didn't settle right with Dany, and she felt Adam's discomfort as well.

Nothing runs that smoothly, that quickly, Adam thought.

"Seems like something we should check out?" Dany asked

him. Underneath his discomfort was curiosity. She ran a hand over his back.

It wouldn't hurt. We haven't traveled up north in quite a while. Best get it done before the weather turns cold.

You're crazy, Adam accused as the storm poured around them. *We should have gone down to the River at the last tunnel entrance.*

Dany didn't waste her time arguing. Lightning crashed overhead, and she slid in the mud, falling to her knees. She was cold and miserable, and it was her own fault. Adam was right. They should have gone underground when they had the chance.

The River was a series of connecting tunnels and walkways developed when the air quality became too polluted before the humans headed for the stars. Some scientists and private funders made safe walkways and communities to contain humanity until they could undo the damage they'd done. But other scientists and private funders decided earth was done for and built ships for the stars. The dream to live among the stars won most people's hearts over living underground, and the funding had gone for spaceships instead of the environmental repairs they'd started. Now the tunnels and subway systems remained in use for travelers.

Dany hated the feel of concrete around her though, and she'd rather travel under the stars. It had been a chance, staying above ground when they had felt the weather turning, but one she'd been willing to risk.

A crash of thunder came too close, and she covered her ears against the noise.

Dany!

She could hear his warning above through the thunder,

but it was too late. The lightning struck a tree near her, and the massive branches split. The branch knocked her to the ground, and she screamed as pain ripped through her left leg.

Adam came running through the mud as she tried to struggle to her feet. He grabbed the back of her pack and pulled, getting her out of the muck, and out from under the branch. Yet she still couldn't get her footing, and he yanked her towards another downed branch. He pulled her over it until she was off her leg and leaning against the wood.

Are you okay? he asked as he came back around and nuzzled at her leg to check the damage.

She whimpered, afraid to pull her pant leg up to look. Blood seeped through the fabric.

I'll be okay. Just find that tunnel entrance! It was the best she could offer Adam. He stared at her, and she dragged her hands through the wet fur around his face and nodded with a grim smile.

I'll make it, she added.

She could feel his concern, but there was nothing else to do. They had to get out of the weather and there was an entrance close by.

Painfully staggering to her feet, she swallowed down her pain and started moving. She didn't know how long she was going or how far she traveled before Adam came to her side and began pushing her towards shelter, but she would never second-guess him. She couldn't see more than three feet in front of her with the rain pouring so hard, but she trusted Adam's sense of direction.

Concrete, grainy and damp, met her hand, and she nearly sobbed with relief. Dany avoided the River whenever she could, but the thought of being able to stop and rest, to get close to a fire and change into warm dry clothes, made up for the stale air and unfamiliar smell tonight.

As Adam led her deeper into the earth and away from the

rain, the sounds of the storm receded. Light flickered ahead from the guard keeping watch on the entrance.

Adam growled as someone approached, but Dany stroked his back and tried to calm him. He was usually better tempered than this, but he always got extra protective when she was hurt.

The man was almost on top of them before Dany's eyes adjusted enough to see him. His eyes were a shade of green that humans were never meant to have. He was a Mod, and she just might be in luck.

"Are you alright?" the man asked.

"Medic?" she asked. He nodded, and she let out a deep breath. "I haven't looked, but my right leg is messed up."

"He gonna let me close?" the man asked, nodding to Adam.

"Adam, you've seen medics before."

Being a medic doesn't make them all kind.

She knew he was right, but she needed the help. "You're fine," she assured the medic.

He came forward and ducked under her shoulder to wrap an arm around her waist and help her forward. "You're lucky it was me on duty tonight."

"Adam would have found you for me. He's a Mod too. He can sense others."

"I meant, I'm from Village 27. We share this watch with Village 26, and they have some funny ideas about Hacks and Mods.

The River had tributaries that ran off it to different regions of the country, and the more popular cities and villages even had hand-painted signposts on the walls to lead the way. In some of the open connecting tunnels, small villages had popped up. Some people lived their whole lives underground, never going up to see the sun. The tunnel dwellers were a superstitious bunch. Most had been raised on over-inflated tales of raiders on the surface and fairytales of the above ground that hadn't been true for decades.

The medic led them to a tent down a side tunnel.

There's another, Adam warned.

She didn't acknowledge his words, but they'd both known there would be. The other man came running out, an old soldier with a metal arm and a sour face.

"Go watch the entrance," the medic told the man. "This one needs me."

"You just want to get out of the wind," the soldier said, but there was a half-smile on his face. He nodded to Dany and Adam, keeping close to the wall away from them.

Dany let out a muffled cry as the medic set her down on a mat on the floor. Adam was at her side, purring, trying to sooth her, but there was nothing he could do.

"Just going to cut your pant leg so I can see the damage," the medic said. Adam tensed but kept purring.

"Do you really need to do that?" she asked.

"Some things are better done by hand than nano-tech," he said. "The tech can knit flesh and bone, but it can't reset it. And it leaves scars if not properly prepared. It'll do the job either way, but I've learned a little patience goes a long way."

Dany nodded and ran a hand over Adam's back, feeling her heartbeat slow. He really was calming when he purred like that.

"I think we're good to go ahead with the tech," the medic said after a quick inspection. "It's a short injection, and it'll hurt for a moment. Then they'll take care of all of it. It'll be best if I let them introduce a pain killer. Will you and your friend here let me take you to the village? We have a place you can sleep it off there."

"This is Adam," she said, pointing to the big cat. "So long as you don't hurt me and he knows what you're doing, he'll be fine. He's intelligent."

The medic nodded. "I'm Jacob. It's nice to meet you, Adam. And?"

"Dany."

She screamed as Jacob's fingers turned into needles, and he wrapped them around her leg. He gave her a sympathetic grin as the needles released the tech that would mend her. The nano-tech was in his blood, a modification performed in vitro. Medics had been raised separate from humanity and kept in havens for the rich. But when it came time for their owners to head to the stars, they'd been left behind like all the rest of the Mods. And unlike the rest of them, their modifications were generational. If he had children, they would inherit it.

She felt herself lifted, and Adam purred louder so she could hear him. *He's taking you away from the storm. Someplace warm.*

"Good." She moaned the word more than spoke it. "I'm getting cold."

"That's the shock talking," the medic said.

She felt Adam's concern just before the nano-tech knocked her out.

When Dany woke, she was in a tent in Village 27. Adam was close by, watching her as two of the village children crawled over him. Apparently, their medic had siblings, and after some shy attempts, they learned Adam was more than happy to let them pet his fur and play with him.

Over the next few days, Dany offered trade to the medic for his healing. The medic refused, but his father accepted stories of the Above Ground and news of their travels for the tent for a few nights while Dany healed. And for entertaining the children, the tent owner gave them dinner and passed on more news about the Underground and River.

"I've heard of this place, Home." He scratched his chin as he spoke. "Some venture out from it, but most who go seem to stay. No one speaks ill of it."

It sounds too good to be true.

Dany said as much to the father. He gave a self-deprecating laugh. "I don't know much, but the only thing I've heard about the people running it was that they used to be military. Or at least military trained."

If they were military, that might explain how the place got set up so fast and why it's stabilized so fast.

"You're right," she said to Adam. "The military didn't leave many of their own behind, though."

When technology had surged ahead, and Mods and Hacks became popular, the military had held back. Too many had argued that Hacks could be hacked themselves. They didn't allow Hacks into the military service and genetic modifications remained the domain of the private sector.

"Thanks for the info," Dany said to the father after several days of questioning when it was clear he knew no more about Home. "I think we'll turn in. We'll be off early in the morning."

They left the village and the medic's family early the next morning. They spent the day walking the River and that night slept curled together against the tunnel walls. The next day, they came across the tunnel opening and took it up to see if the skies had cleared. Clouds still covered the sky, but the ground was dry, and they could walk in the fresh air. Adam ran ahead to scout, stretching his legs. Within a few minutes, he came back to report he'd found a small orchard, laden with apples. She pulled a mesh bag from her pack and filled it with apples, munching as she walked at a leisurely pace. If she couldn't eat them all, she was sure they would run across someone willing to trade for them.

A few hours into their journey, Adam bounded to her side, hackles raised and tension vibrating through his body.

There's another ahead, he said.

"Another what?" Dany lowered her voice when she asked.

Another like me.

"There were no others like you. None of the others survived."

I remember what it felt like when there were. There is another. It's weak but there.

It seemed unlikely, but she wasn't about to doubt Adam. Although other experiments had taken place after the failed experiment that resulted in her bond with Adam, none of the bonded—the animals and people—were the same as her and Adam. Perhaps if they'd had more time, the scientists would have made the telepathic bond work in a way that wouldn't kill them to sever. But the rumor was the scientists who had overseen that particular experiment had left Earth on one of the last shuttles. In all Adam and Dany's searching— and they had searched the original labs heavily after the Exodus—there had been no information about others like them.

"What's your call?" If he wanted to run away from it, she would, but she doubted her companion could turn away from his curiosity.

We have to see, don't we?

"We don't," she told him. "We don't owe anyone anything."

Yeah, well, I'm curious. Aren't you?

She smiled as she ran a hand over the smooth fur of his neck. "You know I am."

Stay close. And be careful. The feeling of the bond is weak, but that doesn't mean the animal is.

It was a warning he didn't need to give, but she appreciated the way he took care of her. She patted his head in a show of understanding, then stood back as he took the lead. They crept through the trees, careful of fallen leaves and branches that may telegraph their movements. The less noise they could make, the better.

After a few minutes, Adam stopped and looked back at her with his startling blue eyes, and she hurried to his side. He lowered himself and began to painstakingly pick his way forward. She stooped down, wishing he would've told her what he'd heard, but she didn't want to distract him now.

A cry rang out into the air. They froze.

It sounded like a child. A human child.

Adam sprang towards the sound and Dany ran with him, their feet crunching the leaves. No time for silence now. They entered a small clearing and Dany saw an older man lying against a tree trunk. Blood covered him, some stains from days ago, but some newer. Somehow, he'd hurt himself or been attacked and bled out slowly. His eyes were closed, but there was no movement of breath. This had been his final rest. His arm was extended, and his hand rested gently on white fur.

Another cry rent the air, and Dany realized the animal with the white fur was a kitten. Adam moved forward, and the white kitten stared up at them with icy blue eyes, watching. She could sense the kitten was modified like Adam. After a second, the kitten moved, and Dany saw a child hiding behind it.

"What the hell?"

Who would do this? Who would experiment on a child and kitten?

Dany tried not to think about it. "Hey kid, are you okay?" she asked.

The child ignored her and moved to hide behind the kitten. Dany moved to the other side and looked at the old man. There was a pack on his back, likely filled with gear for the child. Whoever he was, he'd been trying to care for the kitten and child.

"What the hell am I supposed to do with a kid?" Dany asked.

What the hell am I supposed to do with a kitten?

Dany let out a deep breath and sat on the grassy terrain beside Adam. "Can you talk to him at all?" she asked.

The kitten suddenly perked up its head and sat up.

It's not the same as speaking with you. It's more like I can sense what it feels. And I can make it sense what I feel.

"So, you can let it know that we don't mean it any harm? Or the kid?"

I tried. The kitten is young. I don't know how much she's understanding, but I think I'm getting through to her.

Dany moved slowly forward then and put her hand out so the kitten could see her movements clearly. She smiled and kept her voice calm. When she reached to touch the child, the kitten growled.

"I think I've been warned," she said, trying to keep her voice steady. The kitten was no match for either of them, but it had made its intentions understood clear enough.

Adam purred his response, and even if he didn't say anything else, she could feel his approval of the kitten's actions.

From that angle, she could see that the child was waiting for some sign to act. When the kitten sat back on her haunches, the girl looked up at Dany. "You're like me?" she whispered, sitting up and reaching her hand up to touch Dany's temple, where the scientist had placed one of the implants ten years ago. Dany saw a similar implant on the girl's head.

"Yes, my name is Dany." She pointed back to her companion. "And that is Adam."

"I'm Selene." The kitten growled beside the child, and she

giggled. "It is my name!" The kitten bumped against her, and Selene looked back at Dany. "Doctor called me Silly. So does Terra."

"This would be Terra?" she asked, holding her hand out to the kitten. The kitten head-butted against it softly.

"How old are you, Silly?"

"Five."

"How long have you been with Terra?"

"Last year."

Terra doesn't remember anything except the girl. The kitten was a newborn when they were bonded.

"Who the hell did this?"

The man with her? Or maybe he was getting her away from them?

"Grandpa," she said, pointing to the dead man beside her. "I don't know his name. He said to call him Grandpa. We lived somewhere else. They asked if I wanted a pretty kitty to play with, and they gave me Terra. They were going to take her away though, so Grandpa helped us run away."

Did they start the experiments again? Why?

Dany was furious at the thought. Sure, there were other experiments with Mods and Hacks going on, but no one experimented on the telepathic bonds between humans and animals anymore. Least not that she'd heard of. It was too complicated without the fancy machinery and computers the scientists had taken to the stars. How could someone map out the complex neural system with the basic equipment the scientists had left behind?

"I don't like this," she said to Adam.

"Grandpa got hurt. He said to keep going west and don't stop 'til you get to the ocean. And hide. Don't stay with people or the others would find us." Silly said. "I don't want the people to find us, but I couldn't wake Grandpa up this morning."

"Were you with Grandpa in a village? In the Rivers?"

"We were at Home."

She looked at Adam and sighed. "Guess Home was too good to be true."

If anyone from the military survived, and they found equipment for bonding humans and animals again, they'd want to take advantage of it. If they found any of the scientists or someone who could repeat the experiments, it means trouble. This kid and kitten are trouble for us.

Dany closed her eyes and pressed the heel of her hand between them to soothe out the sudden headache. "What are you saying?" Adam didn't answer right away, but the child was silent. Dany looked back at her. "Can you hear what he's saying to me?"

Silly shook her head. "No, but I can feel it when Adam is talking."

That's good news, at least, Adam said. *And I'm not saying anything, except that... we've stayed out of trouble and managed on our own for a long time.*

"Yeah. We could still manage with them, though."

If people started doing these experiments and then they find out about us, they'll come looking. We need to go deep and not come back out.

"So, you're saying take them with us?"

Well, we can't leave them behind.

"We don't want to go back to the people," Silly said. "Please. We'll keep up. We can be fast!"

There was no way a five-year-old could keep pace with Adam. Hell, Dany slowed him down, and she was used to walking long miles on few rations. But he appreciated the girl's strength and will. That, more than anything, would help her survive.

She isn't alone. We'll take care of her.

She rolled her eyes at Adam. He was apparently a big softy

under all that fur and muscles and teeth and claws. "Just remember you said that when they come looking for her," she told him. To Silly, she smiled. "Don't you worry about that. Fast isn't as good as efficient. Move well. Be careful. Broken bones will ruin you far quicker than a slow pace. But we do need to get away from here. Have you eaten today?"

The girl shook her head.

"I have a real treat for you," she said as she reached down to pick up the five-year-old. Adam watched, and she felt the purr of approval when she set the child on his back. "You get to be the first person to ever ride on Adam's back!"

"Really?" Silly leaned close and wrapped her arms around Adam's neck and stroked his fur eagerly.

"And here," she pulled out a fresh apple for her and a bag of jerky as well. She gave them to Silly. "Eat some of that jerky, but share it with the cats too," she said. "When we find camp tonight, I'm sure Adam will find a good place for him and Terra to hunt, but Adam likes jerky sometimes."

It's not Friskies.

Dany laughed and explained the joke to Silly, but the little girl didn't know about pet food and convenience stores and all of that. "Go on ahead, Adam. I'll be right behind you."

He walked with a sure, steady gait, and the girl had no problem staying on. They might have to come up with some sort of harness if they found themselves in rougher territory. At least until the girl could fend for herself. Terra ran at Adam's side, taking double the steps to keep up with his long strides.

Dany went back to where the old man was sitting up against the tree. "I don't know who you were, Grandpa, but thank you for getting that girl out of there. You did the best you could. We'll take care of both of them from here."

She gently pulled him forward and unhooked the pack from his back. There were clothes for the girl and some basic medical supplies, along with a pouch of food and a container for water.

But the real find was an electric device that looked like the satellite phones soldiers used to carry but with a smooth mirrored surface Dany could see her reflection in. Wires stuck out of the digital mirror screen in strange places, held together in the casing with tape and makeshift coverings. When she turned it on, the reflective screen morphed into a map of the region. She pressed a button to zoom in on her location. When she did, two lights lit up where she was standing, one red and one blue.

A locater device of some kind? A way to track Silly and Terra? She turned it off and shoved it into her pack. Finally, she examined the old man's pack, noting no damage or blood. Dany repacked the bag with a change of clothes for the girl, a few food items, and the water container. The girl needed a pack of her own.

When she reached Adam, he was resting a few miles north, lapping water from a small stream. Dany filled her water and the water container in the second pack without breaking her silence.

Well?

Silly watched Terra at the water's edge a few feet away from them. Dany smiled at her before she looked back at Adam. "The old man only had a few supplies, but he had a device. I think it was for tracking her."

Why would he need that?

"I'm thinking they were developing it. Or he was. He obviously helped her escape, so he either had a change of heart, or he wasn't one of the scientists who bonded Silly and Terra. There were many people that were part of the program. Maybe he was one of the technicians or doctors that stayed behind for some reason?" She shrugged. "I thought they all went to the stars, but maybe some of them stayed. Maybe he wanted to make sure he could find Silly and Terra if they got separated out here?"

Why not just destroy it?

"What if I need to find her?"

He growled softly, but she patted his shoulder as he looked over at the girl and kitten. "I didn't say I was going to try to lose them."

We should keep moving.

"Come on, Silly. Let's get you back up there."

Dany had to pull out some lines and tie the old man's backpack straps together in a weird configuration, but she got it small enough for Silly's back and shoulders. Now if something happened, at least Silly had her own clothes and a few days of food on her back.

As they walked, Adam traveled along the side of the stream. It was leading northeast, and she knew of a few places they could camp for the night; places that might afford them some safety. They could talk about where to go next after Silly and Terra were asleep.

"Silly, can you tell me about your bond with Terra?" Dany asked.

"Uh huh."

Dany laughed as she realized Silly was waiting for more questions. "How do you communicate with him?"

"I just think what I want him to hear."

"Do you hear Terra in words, or emotions, or images?"

She looked at Dany like she might lose her mind. "Words. Isn't that how you do it?"

Crazy lady, how else would it work? Adam chimed in. Dany laughed as she let the line of questioning go.

While they walked, Dany talked about things that Silly

needed to do now that they were traveling together. Things like going nowhere alone, not her or Terra. Adam or Dany needed to be with them at all times while they were learning how to survive.

As the afternoon sun waned, they came across an old city. Adam and Dany had been there before, but just because it had been abandoned and safe then didn't mean it still was. Yet, there was no smoke from campfires in the skyline, and that meant they were probably safe, at least for the night. They couldn't afford to stay any longer, though; they needed miles between them and this Home Silly had come from.

"Sniff us out a good place?" Dany asked Adam.

I'll take the kitten with me. No time like the present to start his training.

Dany smiled at the protectiveness that had already formed in Adam's interactions with Terra. She helped Silly off Adam's back and the giant cat ran off, the white fluffy cat sprinting to keep up.

"Why are you smiling?" Silly asked her.

"Adam would be a good dad," she said. "I didn't expect that."

"He doesn't take care of you?"

"Always, but we take care of each other."

"Terra didn't want to leave me."

Dany knelt down. "Right now, we're on the run. Those men that hurt Grandpa could still be out there looking for you. So, we need to be safe, and that means traveling fast and finding good hiding places. Right now, the two of us are just out in the open where anyone could see us."

It wasn't entirely true, Dany reflected. They had stopped on a hilltop, but had walked down the slope a little, so the tall grasses around them would mostly camouflage them. Silly didn't understand that yet though, and Dany needed to impress upon the child how to stay safe. And quickly.

"So, Adam is going to find us a safe place for tonight, and he's teaching Terra how to do it," Dany continued. "When we're safe, and we can start training you, Adam and I will both start doing it. You both need to know how to survive out here. That's why we set some rules as we were walking, right?" she asked.

"But you'll teach me too? How to hunt and scavenge and all that?"

"We will. What would happen if I broke a leg or something? You'd need to help Adam while I was healing, right?"

Silly's blue eyes got wide, and she nodded. "Of course. I could help."

Adam came bounding up the hillside then. He stopped halfway and waited for Terra to catch up, then walked back to them. Silly flung her arms around the small cat, and Dany shared a look with Adam. He might not say anything, but she could feel the affection running through their own bond. When the two parted, Dany took Silly's hand, and they followed the cats together.

Adam led them away from the houses close by and took them to an old storefront. They hadn't stayed here the last time they'd come through, but this seemed like a good choice. A lot of these places were empty, but you never knew what you could find still in storerooms.

They circled the building, and Dany paused. Behind a few cars in the parking lot were two dead bodies, but Adam didn't seem too interested. When she stopped to inspect them, he paused for a second. *They were living inside before they died. I can still smell them. There are no other people inside.*

She couldn't tell how they died, but their skin was leathery and sunken, and there were no packs on the bodies, meaning they either weren't fleeing or others had looted their bodies. If Adam couldn't smell anyone, then the building and the surrounding area were safe. Adam led them towards the back, past a set of doors with hanging plastic and into a storeroom.

Oh, looky here. Adam stood on two paws and nudged a crate high on a shelf in the storeroom. Dany craned and started laughing.

Tears fell over her cheeks as she reached up into a crate and pulled out a damn box of cat treats. "You and your Friskies. Was there any human food here, or did you just bring us just for this?"

Terra needs Friskies too.

She laughed as she tossed the box on the ground and watched Adam place one giant paw on the edge and rip it open with his teeth. Adam looked up at her expectantly, and she sighed before she grabbed a second box and threw it next to it. Terra pounced. He wasn't near big enough to tear it as easily as Adam, but he worked steadily until the box had a hole in one end. Terra cautiously nibbled on the contents.

"He likes it!" Silly called out in glee.

"I'm getting you a backpack to carry your own Friskies!" Dany told Adam. His only response was to lie on the floor with his box and purr contentedly with Terra beside him. She rolled her eyes but pulled what looked like three storage crates of cat food down and tossed them on the floor. There was plenty for them to eat their fill and leave some for later. Adam and Terra, at least, would feast tonight.

"Come on, Silly, let's see if we can find any human grub around here."

Silly followed her away from the cats with a big grin as they went out into the main store, practically skipping through the empty aisles. She always stayed close, though. Grandpa's death, more than Dany's words, had probably cemented that safety measure in her mind. Dany bent over to look beneath the shelves. Nothing. She even climbed up on top of the shelves to see if anything was left, but others had picked this place clean.

Dany and Silly came around the side of the store where the baby clothes were, and Dany grabbed the little girl's hand and pulled her to a stop. She put a finger to her lips and pushed the girl behind her.

In the middle of the kid's clothing area was a tent. She heard claws clacking across the slick floor, but when Adam came up beside her, he bumped his head into her side and nearly knocked her over.

I told you they lived here.

He pushed her one more time for good measure, making her stumble and left to go back to his Friskies. Silly laughed.

"Yeah, just wait until Terra is big enough to knock you around," Dany teased.

Dany flipped the tent flap open and together they examined the interior. There was a lantern inside and two sleeping bags. On one side were six large crates stacked up in two columns. Dany grabbed the top one and pulled it to the floor, popping it open. Canned food!

"Come eat with me, Adam!" Dany yelled back towards the cats.

Silly watched her and frowned. "Do you have to speak out loud to him?" she asked.

"No, but I go a long time without seeing people sometimes. I don't want to forget to speak. Some places aren't friends to Hacks or Mods. It's best when you meet people to cover up your tech. Lots of good people in the world do crazy things when they feel pushed into a corner."

Silly nodded. "Like stealing me from Home?"

"Yeah, probably like that. Grandpa thought he was helping you. What do you think?" As she asked, she popped open a can and found it was still good. She dumped it into one of the bowls in the tent and handed the peaches to Silly. The next was a can of peas.

"He said they were going to take Terra from me. He said it wouldn't work, and we'd be hurt."

"So, you ran away with him?"

Silly nodded, and Dany ran her fingers through the girl's brown hair. "Same thing happened to us. They were supposed to end the bond between us. I was sick that day though, so we couldn't go in. The other girls and their cats all died. I was lucky. Adam and I started running then, so they couldn't do it to us. And we'll protect you and Terra. Make sure you get to stay together, too."

Adam and Terra came out of the back with their boxes of treats. Adam had piled three in a larger box and was dragging it, but Terra was trotting proudly beside him with a single box.

They sat beside the tent and began to eat again. "You should really look for something more than Friskies," Dany teased. "Those were meant for much smaller cats."

There are plenty of rodents to catch tonight. I'll see what the kitten knows about hunting once the light falls. You wouldn't want us to ruin your appetite.

Like they hadn't eaten raw meat side by side during their worst days when the hunts were scarce, and she was too starved to wait for fire and roasting.

Have you found anything out about Home yet?

Silly had the bowl of peaches turned up and was drinking the syrupy juice as Dany watched her. She handed her the peas and reached for another can. "Adam wants to know about Home."

Silly set her bowl down and leaned over against Terra, who nuzzled against her. "I had a nice room and lots of food. But after I got Terra, they wouldn't let me talk to anyone or play with anyone."

"Did you always live there?"

She shook her head. "No, I lived in Village 23. They came and said they could take us, the kids with no family. Some of the adults came with us, and they saw we were safe, and they went back home."

"Did you stay safe?"

"Uh-huh. I got to take a warm bath and eat warm food. And I got to learn to read books. And every day I got to go outside and play on a swing! But some of the kids stopped coming outside. Maybe they were like me. Maybe they got a cat too?"

Dany smiled at the girl, but she had a sinking feeling in her stomach. "Maybe."

"Everyone was nice there, but there were some places we weren't allowed to go. And there were a lot of rules. And if you broke the rules, you had to leave, so everyone was afraid of the rules."

"I'm very glad Grandpa got you out and brought you to us."

Silly nodded. "He said there was another. He said she was the only one to trust. He was looking for you and him."

Dany's heart dropped into her stomach. "What?"

"Grandpa said if he couldn't find you, we had to run. But he had the funny mirror. He used to look at it when he was walking. He said it would find you."

Realization sunk in. *The device wasn't to track Silly and Terra. He'd found a way to track us.*

Her mind rushed with the implications. If they knew where she was—

They'd have come already if they knew, Adam said, to calm her. *You saw what they'd left behind in the labs. There were no records. Grandpa had to have been part of the original experiments. And he knew our link was never broken. Maybe he took the girl when he did because we were coming closer? Or to keep us from going to them and being discovered?*

"You think he was saving us both?"

I think someone found a way to hide us from them all those years ago. I have a little faith that a man who died to protect a little girl, put his life on the line for another girl and her cat ten years ago.

Not so sure I can take that leap of faith with you, but whoever he was, I'm glad he got Silly out. "When did you get so sentimental?" Dany asked aloud.

There are Friskies involved. I'm not responsible.

Dany laughed and reached for Silly, who threw herself into her arms.

That night, the tent was almost too warm, but Dany wouldn't have left it for anything. She had Silly snuggled up against her side, and Terra pressed behind the girl. And Adam, as always, was at her back as she rested her head on him.

You haven't had a family in a long time.

"I have you," she whispered. "That's always been enough."

He purred his agreement, but as she fell asleep, she heard one more thought slither through. *This is nice, though.*

As nice as the setup was, they couldn't afford to stop moving. They found a backpack better fitted for Silly and filled it with light foodstuffs. She had a water container attached with a carabiner on the outside of the pack and a fresh set of clothes on the bottom. Dany's own pack was heavier than it had been in a while, but she was more than happy to have the extra food with them.

They stopped to eat when they crossed a small stream and found a clearing to rest for a while. Dany was used to long days of traveling, but Silly wasn't, and Terra was flagging as he tried to keep up with Adam's larger strides.

Be calm, was the only warning Dany had before Adam ran

away. She automatically grabbed a beanie from a side pocket on her pack and pulled it over her head to cover her implant.

"He'll be back," she whispered to Silly. "If anyone comes, don't speak. And both of you do exactly what I say."

Soldiers. It's too late to run. Stay where you are. Keep them talking.

Dany stiffened but pulled Terra to sit between her and Silly. They only had a few minutes before Dany heard the snap of branches underfoot. She looked up across the small stream and saw three men with guns pointed at her. Another came up from behind them and smiled.

Why are you scared?

Adam must have felt the moment she recognized the man across from her. She'd never forget the doctor who had put the implant in her head. He had the same smile that didn't reach his eyes; one brown and one blue. The infamous Dr. Phillip Days. Why hadn't he gone to the stars with the others? Had something happened?

"You've put us on a merry chase, Selene," Dr. Days said. "It's time to come home now."

"Are you with her?" Dany asked, trying to swallow her fear. Had Dr. Days recognized her? She pulled the beanie down lower. "I was really worried. I found her wandering alone in the woods with this cat, and I didn't know what to do with her. So, I just took her with me, hoping someone would find us." She was babbling, but hopefully the scientist would just think they'd startled her.

She swallowed against the lump in her throat and ran a hand through Silly's hair to keep herself calm. Adam must have been calming Terra as well, because the white cat was sitting as docile as could be beside her. When she ran a finger over his back, she could feel how tense the kitten was.

"Selene went on a walk with one of our people," Dr. Days started, his eyes crinkling in the corners with a fake smile. "But he was injured, and she must have run off. We've been worried about her."

It had been over ten years since she'd seen Dr. Days, and those had been hard years, but it was obvious the scientist didn't recognize her. Well, she'd never been more than an experiment to him.

"Why don't you have a seat? We've been walking all day, and Selene should probably eat before she goes home. Where is that, by the way?" Dany asked. "Looking for any new people?"

Dr. Days nodded as he jumped across the small stream and sat on the ground opposite Dany. She tried not to recoil. The soldiers stayed where they were but had put their guns down. "We have a place called Home, just a two-day walk from here. We're always looking for skilled people. If you're out here on your own, you must know a thing or two."

Dany smiled, "Oh, I get by."

Silly is going to run. Don't let them follow.

Terra growled softly at her side, then pounced after a bug in the air. She pounced further away from them and took off running.

"Terra!" Silly ran after him. The men were startled, but Dany stood and smiled. "She's just getting the cat. No need to get worked up. Her backpack is still here."

She could feel Adam though, running, flexing his legs, his haunches bunched. Their plan was in action! Dany slid her backpack off and swung it at Dr. Days, knocking him to the ground. Adam roared into the clearing, but Dany didn't stay to watch. She ran after Silly, catching up to the girl and kitten. Silly jumped onto her back, and Dany grabbed Terra and ran.

She could feel the fight through Adam, feel his satisfaction as he took his prey, his joy at protecting what was his. There was pain but nothing so great that the cat was concerned.

When she felt his relief, she stopped running and let the other two down.

"Dany?" Silly asked, her eyes wide with terror.

"Adam is coming. It's safe now."

It was a tense fifteen minutes as Dany watched the woods in silence. Silly was petting Terra, but then she'd get worried and reach up to touch Dany's leg and start petting her, too. It was kind of cute.

When the big cat finally made it to them, Dany ran her hands over his fur, looking for what had hurt him.

I got knocked into a tree. It wasn't a weapon.

She was surprised that his face was wet, but she could only see a tint of blood there. Before she could ask, he dropped onto the forest floor and let Dany look at his back quarters. She couldn't see anything, but she could feel how tense the muscles were. "Are you really okay?"

He bumped his head into hers and nuzzled against her face. She smelled swamp water.

We're safe. None of the men escaped. Dr. Days won't do it to anyone else. He's gone.

There were sure to be other scientists who would try, but at least they had that. And Silly and Terra were still safe, for the moment at least. Silly watched, but when Dany smiled at her, the little girl ran forward and threw herself at the big cat.

I didn't mean to scare you. I needed to clean up before I came back. I didn't want the child to see the blood.

Dany hadn't thought of it, but she realized then he was right. "Warn me next time."

No more next times. Let's never do that again.

She wrapped her arms around his neck and Silly giggled. "Agreed."

That night, they camped in a cave, warm and well-fed.

We'll go inland. Fewer people. Fewer cities. Until they're old enough to take care of themselves, we'll take them there.

"And if the scientists follow us there, too?"

They'll stop, or they'll all die. They modified me, made me bigger and smarter and more protective. And then they bonded us. They made us Hacks, but they also made us family. My life for yours, Dany. Our bond is forever.

Dany closed her eyes and let out a deep sigh as she relaxed against Adam. "My life for yours, Adam. Bonded forever."

Reflections Of Hawthorne

By Donna Keeley

"Do you need help, Mom?" Maggie offered, as her mother tread slowly up the front steps. "It's been a long day."

"Yes, it has," Jennifer Thompson agreed wearily. The funeral for her mother, Maggie's grandmother, had been long, with many speeches and remembrances. The hot afternoon sun beating down on people like her, wearing black at the graveside service, was the last obstacle to overcome on a very emotional day. All during the reception at the church, she'd felt wrung out.

Maggie stood by the open door to let her mother through, while holding packages and cards from the many friends and family members who attended. The late Helen Wilder was well-known and well-liked in this small town just north of Los Angeles. Many of the parcels were mementos that kind-spirited people thought Maggie, or her mother, would appreciate. But today, they were more reminders of their lost loved one rather than objects of comfort.

With the door shut behind her, Maggie placed everything haphazardly on the central dining table. "Let me get you a glass of cold water, and then I'll go upstairs and start a bath," she said.

Jennifer sat down heavily at the table. "That sounds nice. Although a glass of wine would be better." She grinned, though it was tinged with sadness.

Maggie smiled back. "Of course. I'll even join you." She kicked off her dress shoes and walked into the kitchen to get the drinks. She returned shortly with a red for her mother and a white for herself. The two women drank in silence.

A sleek black and white tuxedo cat hopped onto the table, sitting gracefully while wrapping his tail around him, contemplating the two women with wide amber eyes. Maggie reached out to scratch his cheek.

"I'm sure you're lonesome, aren't you Hawthorne," she sympathized.

"My mother and her tuxedo cats," commented Jennifer. "And all named Hawthorne. I used to think she was senile at an early age and just called them all the same name because she could remember it." She chuckled, then brushed her hand over Maggie's hand on the table.

"Don't worry about the bath, pumpkin," Jennifer told Maggie. "I think I'll just go to bed. It's been a long day."

"Alright. Goodnight, Mom."

Maggie took the wine glasses back to the kitchen, washed them out, and left them in the drying rack. This old 1930s home never came with an automatic dishwasher, and her grandmother kept it that way. Maggie's mother, a child of the 60s, couldn't wait to get out on her own and make use of the late twentieth-century technology. Their family refrigerator with ice and water on the door had been a big deal to Jennifer. Maggie smiled, thinking about it. She knew her grandmother had wanted to die here, but fate had other plans. A long fight with cancer, and then a four-month stay in a care center at the very end because her needs were more than the family could provide.

Jennifer had moved back in during those last two years, after her own husband, Maggie's father, had died of a sudden heart attack. It was a shock to both mother and daughter, and Maggie had encouraged her mother to move in. She recalled many summers spent here during her childhood, running up and down the stairs, playing in the backyard, blowing dandelions, and making grass blade whistles.

As a child, Maggie had free rein of the house except for one room—her grandmother's bedroom. Helen had even kept it locked for protection, telling Maggie there were things in there she didn't want broken accidentally. At the time, Jennifer had scoffed a bit, defending her daughter by saying she was very responsible, but Helen hadn't budged. Being a compliant child, Maggie had accepted the rule. She'd felt no temptation to try and sneak into her grandmother's bedroom, and as she got older, it mattered less and less with her own life to cultivate.

Maggie turned out all the downstairs lights and made her way up the stairs, finding it ironic she was sleeping in the very room her grandmother had barred her from as a child. It had all seemed so silly from a woman who was very intelligent, a skillful painter, and a loving relative. Helen's life had been good and, judging by the speeches from her friends this afternoon, she'd been well-respected. A few tears escaped as Maggie climbed, and she didn't notice the black and white shadow following her.

The next few days were busy ones. Cleaning out the rooms of her grandmother's possessions was a Herculean effort. Maggie's mother had done some sorting during the months Helen was in the facility, but the garage and attic required more effort, so she had waited until Maggie arrived. A couple of neighbors stopped by and generously helped Maggie and Jennifer move the large trunks from the attic to the back porch. Maggie spent hours going through them, finding vintage dresses from her great grandmother during her Hollywood actress days. Age and insect infestation had destroyed many of them, but the few salvageable ones Maggie wrapped carefully in old sheets so she could bring them home for restoration and display.

The last room to clear was her grandmother's bedroom. Maggie and Jennifer removed the clothes from the antique wardrobe and started on the drawers of the tall dresser. Nearly done, Maggie reached down to open the bottom drawer, but it resisted her efforts.

"I can't get this one open," sighed Maggie.

"Probably locked," Jennifer said, after trying it herself. "Mom had her secrets, although I never knew what they were. We can deal with it later; maybe get a screwdriver in there and break it open."

"How about calling a locksmith?" Maggie suggested. "This dresser is so beautiful; I'd hate to ruin it. And if you want to sell it, it'll be worth more intact."

"True," her mother agreed. "I'm just tired and want this over, I guess." She sat heavily on the edge of the bed. Maggie sat beside her and rubbed her mother's back. "It's going to take some work to get this house in shape to sell."

"You're really going to sell it?"

"This wasn't really my home, growing up. Mom had her paintings, her art friends, her museum job, and Dad was at the office all the time. I spent more time at my friends' houses than here. I know you have memories of visiting during the summer, but it was only one week out of the year."

"I know," Maggie replied, nodding. "It's just that it's been in the family for so long."

"Well, there are still some medical bills to pay. I'd offer it to you, but you're established in New York with your fancy master's in art history degree, and I don't think you're ready to give all that up to move out here, so I need to sell it. You can understand that. Plus, I'm ready to move to Palm Springs to start my single senior life," she smiled, and her daughter returned the smile.

"Fair enough. Let's pick up in here and then go out for some dinner," Maggie suggested. "I think we need a break after all this work."

After returning home from dinner, both women headed for bed. It had been a tiring day, both physically and emotionally. As Maggie settled in between the sheets, she glanced at the dresser with the locked drawer. Hawthorne was in his usual spot, lying on the handmade lace doily covering the top. Her glance moved to look at the ornate mirror that hung over the dresser. The frame, composed of gold, silver, copper, and brass, was an amazing example of the Art Deco period. It was her grandmother's most prized possession, aside from the cats she had over the years. Maggie had even written about it for her thesis.

It had belonged to Helen's mother, Marie, who had been a minor starlet in the 20s and 30s but caused a scandal by getting pregnant while unmarried and refusing to give up the baby. Since she wasn't a major lead at the studio, they'd easily discarded her. The mirror was supposedly associated with her lover, but Marie had never revealed who he was and took the secret to her own grave. It was a credit to her great-grandmother's tenacity that she raised Helen on her own and never married. Helen appeared unaffected by having no father in her life, but it made sense that if the mirror belonged to him, it would indeed be a precious memento. Even in her last months with her faculties failing, Helen had chanted, "Save the mirror. Keep it safe. Don't lose the mirror."

"The mirror is safe, Grandma," Maggie said to the empty room.

"She knows, darling," came a male voice from the dresser.

Maggie startled and sat up in bed. The tuxedo cat was now sitting on his spot, looking at her thoughtfully.

"Did you... speak?" She looked at the cat incredulously.

"Not in that form, I'm afraid. Come look in the mirror, Maggie," the voice invited. "I've been waiting for an opportunity to talk with you."

Not understanding, she pushed back the covers, got out of the high bed, and crept cautiously up to the mirror. Instead of her own reflection, she saw a dapper-looking man staring back at her. His light brown hair was wavy, the pencil mustache neatly trimmed, and although she could only see him from the chest up, he appeared to be wearing a tuxedo from the 1930s but without the top hat. The man smiled widely at her. His brown, twinkling eyes captivated Maggie. He was every inch a leading man from her great-grandmother's era.

"And you are?" she asked cautiously, still not sure what was going on. Was she dreaming? She felt very much awake right now.

"Hawthorne Radcliffe. I am delighted to make your acquaintance." He bowed dramatically.

Hawthorne, Maggie thought. Maybe that's why her grandmother's cats were all named Hawthorne, in some sort of remembrance to this man.

"How do you know who I am? And why are you here? Or rather, in there?" She gestured to the mirror.

"You are my dear Helen's granddaughter, Margaret," he answered simply. "Although you prefer to be called Maggie. But before I explain more, I need you to promise me something."

"Okay." Maggie said slowly, figuring dream-promises weren't binding if she was indeed dreaming.

The smile disappeared, and his voice was rough with emotion. "Once I'm done telling you my story, I want you to break the mirror." Maggie saw a single tear track down his cheek.

"But I promised Grandma I would keep it safe," she countered.

"And you have kept it safe during her time on this plane," he replied. "But she's gone now, and that contract is broken. I know you don't understand right now, and I want to tell you everything, but I must have your promise first. Please, Maggie."

Maggie could feel his desperation, even through the glass. "Alright," she said solemnly. "I agree."

Another tear leaked out. "Thank you, my dear. You are making the right decision, believe me. But before I start, I need you to take out the items in the bottom drawer."

"It won't open," Maggie replied. "We tried when we cleaned out this dresser."

"Do you see the metal ornament in the center of the drawer?" he asked.

"Yes."

"Slide it."

Squatting, Maggie grabbed the ornament and rotated it, revealing a keyhole. "Wow. We didn't even notice that."

"You weren't supposed to," he replied with a smile.

"But where is the key?" she asked, standing.

Hawthorne in the mirror glanced at Hawthorne the cat, who pawed at a corner of the lace doily underneath him, pulling it up and revealing a very flat small key. The cat looked at Maggie as she picked up the key.

"Mom did say Grandma had many secrets. Does Mom know about you?"

The man shook his head. "She could never see me. Only those with an artist's soul can see what is unbelievable. Your mother is very grounded, in fact, and can't contemplate the fanciful."

"True. As a nurse, she believed in science above all else; such a difference from artsy Grandma," Maggie smiled. Squatting again, she opened the locked drawer and removed a polished wooden box with a detailed Art Deco motif carved in the lid. The box itself was an incredible piece of art, made with multiple pieces of different colored wood, to form a striking pattern on the sides and top. It was a testament to the craftsman's skill.

"Put it there." Hawthorne gestured to the right side of the mirror as Maggie stood up with the box. Although the box was twelve inches square, because it was made from wood pieces, it was quite light. She complied with Hawthorne's request and opened the hinged lid.

Inside was a small black photo book, various documents, a few pieces of jewelry, and an unusual chunk of amber with veins of metal running through it.

"I've never seen anything like this," she said, reaching for the amber, her eyes wide.

"Don't touch that!" warned human Hawthorne while the cat slapped her hand.

"Ouch!" She withdrew her hand instantly.

"I apologize for being so abrupt," Hawthorne said from the mirror. "But that stone keeps me here in the mirror. If you touch it, you'll be trapped as well."

"Sorry," Maggie apologized, chastised.

"Let me tell my tale so we can satisfy your curiosity," he said. "And don't forget your promise to break the mirror."

Maggie nodded.

"Pull out the photo book," he instructed.

Careful to avoid the dangerous stone, she removed the book and then shut the box lid to avoid any accidents. Maggie opened to the first page and saw two grainy black and white images of her great-grandmother as a young woman. Marie was indeed worthy of the starlet title, with her beautiful face, wavy dark hair, lithe body, and a smile that lit up everything around her.

"My beautiful Marie," sighed Hawthorne. "I fell in love with her immediately, despite being already married. I insisted she be in every film I starred in, although she wasn't top billing. Over time, everyone in Hollywood could see she was an amazing actress. She was beautiful, smart, and charming.

"My wife, Anna, and I had married very young, and for good or bad, she could not have children. I never blamed her for that, but she became a very miserable person. The studio would probably have granted me a divorce, but I was still making my way up the ladder to stardom and felt it wasn't time to ask. But as my marriage got worse, Marie became the shining light in my darkness, and I would do anything for her. I bought this house so we could have a place of our own. Turn the page," he instructed.

Maggie complied and saw pictures of the house with Marie standing in front of it, holding an exact copy of the cat sitting on the dresser. A lover's nest. She turned to the next page automatically and saw the remaining items were newspaper clippings and publicity stills of both Hawthorne and Marie, trotted out for their public appearances. She closed the book carefully.

"The studio enjoyed promoting us as a couple. As you can see, we were a good match." He smiled wistfully, remembering. "But like many good things, it wasn't to last.

"To help Anna, I had suggested she join one of the German American societies since her family was German. I genuinely hoped it would be good for her, but it was the worst thing I could have done. It only helped her to become a supporter of the Nazis established here in Los Angeles. And even more frightening were the plans they made to kill people like Louis B. Mayer and Samuel Goldwyn. Those papers in the box are hers, listing some of the horrible ideas they came up with. I know we're not Jewish, but it was, and still is, terrifying." His voice was strained as he spoke.

"I never knew that," Maggie commented softly. "History doesn't say much about Nazis in Hollywood."

"Yes, since they considered Jewish people the enemy, it made sense they would target the powerful studio heads. If only I had paid more attention to these events, I may have had a very different outcome to my life," he admitted sadly. "But I was so infatuated with Marie, and she with me, we became careless. The Hollywood magazines printed many articles about us and the movies we were in together, so it was very easy for my wife to become suspicious. Anna used her network of fellow Nazis to track us, which confirmed that I was having an affair. And I was so caught up in my own happiness, I never noticed. I was just relieved she had something to occupy herself, so I didn't pay attention to her activities."

The man in the mirror shook his head, his eyes closed tightly. "I was such a fool," he chastised himself. "It was spring of 1939 when my wife found this address and caught us both in the house. She was enraged and hysterical. She screamed at Marie, shoving those papers in her face and threatening to have her executed. I pushed Marie behind me to protect her while I yelled at Anna, telling her to leave immediately, and that I wanted a divorce.

"A Romani woman who lived next door and had struck up a friendship with Marie heard the disturbance and came over to see what was going on. What a sight we must have made, three grown adults shouting over each other in the front room, with Anna being the loudest. As the neighbor opened the screen door to let herself in, my wife reached her limit and drew a gun from her purse, aiming it in my direction. I moved forward to disarm her when she fired at me from point-blank range. The women all screamed in panic, and my wife, realizing what she had done, dropped everything and fled the house.

"There was no recovery from this wound, and I fell to the floor with my blood soaking into the rug. I still remember my valiant Marie dropping to the ground and holding me in her arms, begging me not to die. And then she gave me the best reason in the world to live; she told me she was pregnant with our child. We were both weeping, me for the child I would never see or meet, and she for losing the man she loved. I told her to let the child go and continue in her career, but she was adamant she would keep the baby and raise it alone. She knew very well she would never act again, but she was resolved. I was so caught up in my grief I almost didn't hear the neighbor woman offer Marie an alternative to losing me."

Maggie was spellbound by his narrative, her mouth agape as he recited these events to her. Hawthorne continued.

"The Romani woman kneeled next to Marie, ignoring the blood, and told her she knew a way to capture my soul to keep it from departing. After that, I lost consciousness. Later, Marie told me the entire story. The neighbor went home and brought back the stone while Marie found a mirror to use. This one. As you saw in the picture, the cat was already part of the house.

"According to Marie, the neighbor chanted something as she waved the stone over my body. Then my body faded away, and my spirit reappeared in the mirror. The cat, who was simply called Cat, became my familiar, his soul attached to mine. This Hawthorne," he nodded toward the cat, now lying in a loaf position with his front feet tucked under him, "is how I move within the world. I see and hear everything through him."

"Wait." Maggie was still processing everything he had said. "This is the same cat?"

"Yes. We have been bound since 1939. Over 80 years ago."

"I... I... I have no words," Maggie stammered, her logical mind trying to comprehend this information. "This seems too fantastical to be real."

"I agree, but I can assure you it is very real. It happened as I have described, and the items in the box prove it."

Leaving the box on the dresser, Maggie sat heavily on the bed. "So, you're my great-grandfather."

"In spirit, yes." He smiled, and the twinkle returned to his eyes.

"But why didn't Marie break the mirror when she was near the end of her life?" Maggie asked. "She could have done it any time."

Hawthorne's face deepened into sadness. "Because my dear daughter wouldn't let her."

"What?" Maggie stood back up so she could see him more clearly.

"Marie lost everything after my death. She refused to abort the child, so the studio fired her. Being a single mother at that time was extremely hard but being able to share our daughter's life was a blessing. As a child, Helen and I played a game we called Man-in-the-Mirror. In those days, children were easily dismissed when they spoke of their father being trapped in the glass. When Helen was old enough to understand, Marie and I explained how I came to be here and how we needed to keep it secret. As she grew and sought her independence, I played less of a role in Helen's life. As it should be, of course.

"The man she married was a hard worker, made a good living, and supported the family. They all lived here, with Marie keeping this room as her own. I watched Jennifer grow up, although she never saw me, which probably was just as well. I watched my beautiful Marie age, and we both dreamt of a release for me so I could join her when she passed. The day after Marie's funeral, I begged my Helen to smash the mirror —but she refused, vowing to never let me go.

"Helen's own marriage was crumbling by this time, and she often used me as support, so I understood her feelings. What child wouldn't want a parent nearby who would never die? But I was and am tired of this limited existence. I want to be with my Marie. I want my imprisonment to end. Helen and I argued over and over during the years, but she would not budge. She added the lock to the bottom drawer to hide the box away from suspicion. And so, I have merely existed these last few decades."

Hawthorne paused with a sigh, and Maggie felt his sorrow. "Some people think an immortal life is a gift but watching everyone you love pass away forever wears on the soul. It is past time..."

The cat interrupted him with an ear-piercing yowl, leaping to his feet and bolting out the door. Suddenly, the room shook violently, the floor pitching back and forth like the deck of a ship in a storm. The house creaked and groaned, and Maggie fell against the bed. She saw the dresser topple over, threatening to crush her, but it got caught on the edge of the mattress, creating a cover for her as pieces of ceiling rained down.

Books and decorations fell from the shelves, smashing onto the floor. Picture frames shattered, spreading glass everywhere, and the entire house creaked in protest as the earth underneath shifted. Maggie choked back a scream as dust rose in great plumes, coating her throat. The horrifying movement seemed to go on forever.

Then, the shaking stopped. There was silence.

"Maggie!" Her mother's frightened call came from the hallway. "Maggie, are you alright?" Jennifer was nearly crying.

"I'm here," she called back through the closed door. "The dresser fell over, but it protected me from the ceiling collapse. I can't move it by myself; I need some help. Be sure to put some shoes or slippers on before coming in. There's a lot of broken glass and ceramic pieces on the floor."

"I'll be right back," Jennifer reassured her daughter.

With effort from the outside, the door bedroom opened, pushing pieces of drywall aside so Maggie's mother could get in. The two of them righted the heavy dresser against the wall.

"Oh no," Jennifer exclaimed, picking up the slightly bent mirror frame with almost all of the glass missing. "Mom's favorite mirror got broken."

"I know a restorer in New York who can repair it," Maggie offered.

Jennifer handed it to her. "You might as well take it. You wrote the paper about it, and I think mom would want you to have it."

"Let's shut off the gas and electricity, then get dressed and wait outside for the authorities," Maggie suggested. "It might be dangerous to stay in here."

In the morning, a county inspector cleared the structure as still safe, despite the interior damage. Other houses on the block had also survived the earthquake, mostly intact. Over the next two days, with help from volunteers and county authorities, most of the mess was cleaned up and hauled away. Except for some of the upstairs ceilings, the place was livable again.

Reluctantly, Maggie approached her mother the evening after the last of the debris was taken away to tell her Maggie needed to return to New York. While working the cleanup, she had spent some stolen moments trying to find Hawthorne the cat, but there was no sign of him.

"I'm so sorry to leave you with this," Maggie apologized to her mother. "I'm also worried about Hawthorne. It's been a couple of days, and he's still missing."

"He'll turn up," Jennifer reassured her. "Or maybe he'll find a new family. I'm not much of a cat person, you know.

And I won't be alone; my friend Beth from Phoenix is coming to help." She smiled.

"You'll be well taken care of," Maggie said with a grin. Beth was her mother's best friend from college.

A day later, Maggie packed her bags to prepare for her flight home. She was standing over the extra suitcase she had bought to carry her great-grandmother's dresses and other heirlooms, contemplating the slightly bent mirror frame with its missing glass, hoping her great-grandfather had finally found his release, even if the earthquake was responsible. Using an old quilt for padding, she carefully wrapped the mirror frame in a quilt and placed it in the suitcase.

When she came to the ornate box from the dresser, she paused, thinking it might be best to remove the magical piece of amber and destroy it, since it was potentially dangerous. Placing the box on the bed, she carefully lifted the lid, but the stone was no longer there. She moved items around, searching but could not find it. However, she found something more intriguing and less intimidating.

As her hands sifted through the items, she heard a soft metallic sound that was definitely not from the jewelry. Pulling out the object, she held it up.

It was a cat collar with a small tag that read HAWTHORNE.

Tears flowed, both happy and sad.

"Rest in peace, Hawthorne."

GRAVE DEMISE
By K. R. Cervantez

Camren screamed as claw-like hands clamped down onto her shoulders.

Her grandfather pulled her back, his thin, boney fingers digging into her skin. Her heart slammed into her throat and blood rushed to her ears. All the air seemed to leave her lungs, and her legs shook as he spun her around.

"Leave it alone!" her grandpa yelled. "Leave her mirror alone! Don't you take it down. She says we need it!" His eyes were glazed over and confused. They flickered as if he was having trouble focusing.

It was not how she remembered Grandpa's eyes.

Camren took a deep breath. She had to take control of the situation before it got even more out of hand.

"Grandpa, you have Alzheimer's. None of this is real. You can't see Granny in the mirror. She's dead. Please, let me take it down." Her voice shook, but her tone was soft. Truth be told, the mirror had started to creep her out. She wanted it gone and not just because she hoped it would help the elderly man.

It had been two months since she'd moved in to help

around the house. The family didn't want old man Lawrence, her grandfather, removed from his beloved home and put in a nursing home. As a freelance editor, her moving in was the best option to keep him in the house he loved. It was days like this she almost regretted her decision, but Grandpa was one of her favorite people. Even now, as he stood in front of her, panting like a rabid animal, all she wanted to do was hug the grieving and confused man.

"Please, Grandpa," she pleaded.

He said nothing. His eyes were empty, as if he were just a shell of himself. She took a step back toward the mirror and placed a hand on the silver frame. For a moment, nothing happened. Grandpa seemed almost lucid as he stared at the mirror. Camren took that as a good sign. She breathed out, her heart slowing.

Then her handsome gray tabby, Ash, launched himself over her grandfather's shoulder and attacked her arm. The cat's claws and teeth sank into her flesh.

She cried out and grabbed Ash by the scruff of his neck. She didn't want to hurt the tabby, but she had to get him off her arm. Despite her screams and tugs, he continued to claw the hell out of her arm, his teeth latched onto her wrist. Blood dripped to the floor as she spun around, trying to get her cat off.

"Ash! Ash, get off! Let go!" she cried out. Movement in the mirror made her look up.

She froze.

She watched the color in her face drain from her reflection. Her eyes bulged. She felt her lips quivering and tasted blood dripping from where her lip ring had been, though she couldn't remember how it had been pulled out. Her dark hair, so much like her grandfathers except for the rainbow streaks, hung lank in her face. As if he knew something she didn't, her grandfather stood behind her, a terrible grin distorting his features.

Those eyes. Oh god, his eyes were dark and dead in the mirror. They had been so full of life just hours ago. Big, green, and framed with laugh lines that showed her how much joy he'd found in life. Though that wasn't even what had her almost pissing in her pants. She held the cat in her arms. She knew she did. She could feel the soft warm fur still struggling in her hands.

But in the mirror, her hands were empty.

Ash had no reflection.

Another scratch appeared on her arm, seemingly made by some invisible demon. It had to be the cat, even if she couldn't see him in the mirror.

The noise that ripped from her throat didn't sound human as she stumbled back from the mirror. Her grandpa caught her shoulders again and said something in a hoarse whisper that she didn't hear. Ash abandoned the attack, jumping onto the bed behind them. He yowled as if daring her to touch the mirror again.

Grandpa let go of her, and she fell against the rocking chair. "Don't go touchin' her mirror again," he said, sounding more like his old self. He shuffled from the room, mumbling something about shelling peas. Such a simple, normal task compared to what had just happened. She watched him disappear from sight before looking over at Ash. The tabby stared at her from the foot of the bed. His tail flicked as he licked his muzzle, his teeth glistening. Camren looked up at the mirror, and even from her position on the floor, she could see the bed in the mirror. Once again the gray tabby didn't have a reflection.

She was going crazy, surely, she was. Camren squeezed her eyes shut, thinking that if she couldn't see it, it wasn't happening. The old man wasn't staring at her like he didn't know her. Her cat wasn't watching her like prey. It made no sense.

Honestly, maybe it was just the house. She had basically grown up in this house, out in the country where the only neighbors were sunflower fields. She had always found stability within these walls. Spending summers here playing dress up in the mirror with Granny, and tending the garden with Grandpa, seemed to renew her soul. The place she'd loved as a child now seemed darker than ever. All the special memories were fading. Replaced with the horror that now surrounded her. Maybe being away from the city lights and technology that actually worked was getting to her. After all, she hadn't lived here for ten years.

Hell, even the garbage truck didn't come out this far, and she could still smell the trash smoldering in the burn pit. The odor made the situation feel so much more dire. It was a distinct bitter smell of burning plastic and old food. It clung to the air, in the house, got into her clothes, into her dreams, as if trying to suffocate her, really setting the mood.

The mirror that hung in the bedroom belonged to her grandmother. She'd always been told there was something special about it, and her cat, Ash, seemed to think so too. Camren always thought it was because the mirror was a family heirloom; something the women in her family had passed down to each other for generations. Grandpa had said her mother would get it and then eventually, Camren would too. She used to relish the idea of one day owning such a beautiful oval mirror. She loved all the silver filigree and how well kept it looked.

But obviously, it was a trigger for her grandfather, and maybe it was making her crazy, too. Maybe there was asbestos in the glass or even LSD seeping out of the frame. There was no way Ash didn't have a reflection. Everything else matched perfectly. She could see the nightstand in the mirror. The old alarm clock that wasn't used anymore was there, too. She could even see the rocking chair her grandmother had died in, still moving from when Camren fell against it. The light lacy curtains, in need of a good dusting, the decorative pillows with floral embroidery; they were all right where they should be in the mirror. She could even see the hand knitted afghan where Ash sat, so why couldn't she see the cat?

As the smell of burning trash hit her again, she got an idea, but she'd have to wait until Grandpa was completely distracted.

She stood up; her legs were unsteady but they held her. Camren made her way to the bathroom and ran her bloody arm under the tap. The scratches and bite marks stung like a bitch. They definitely felt worse than they looked, though she wondered if she should get them looked at. She couldn't believe Ash had done this. Sure, she had rescued him from the streets, but her sweet boy had always been so loving. The best cuddler. Until tonight.

Her body felt feverish, and she couldn't seem to swallow past the tightness in her throat. She let the tears fall, unable to hold them back.

She cried for a long time but eventually calmed down. With one final blow of her nose, Camren went to the living room. Her grandfather was in his chair, the light from the television flickering across his hands, and yes, there was a bowl in his lap where he was putting his shelled peas. Ash was on the floor, lazily playing with one of the shells that hadn't quite made it to the bag. Neither of them looked up at her as she sat down. It was as if the scene in the bedroom hadn't happened.

It couldn't have happened. There was so much going on, and with everything piling up, she had been under a lot of stress. Hell, she'd missed an important editing deadline, and she never forgot things like that. Taking care of her grandfather had been harder than she'd thought it would be.

She leaned back in her chair, fiddling with the lace doily that covered the wear and tear on the arms. The ancient recliner still smelled faintly of sweet tobacco and creaked when she pulled the lever for the footrest. With a sigh she focused on the television screen.

Her favorite characters were talking about forensic evidence on the television bringing more tears to her eyes. Grandpa had started their show without her. It shouldn't have bothered her, especially after what had just happened, but it hurt knowing that he was getting worse and didn't seem to care about her anymore.

She loved him so much, and he was forgetting about her.

The old television flickered in the dark as they sat in strained silence. The T.V. still had a bubbled screen and high definition was certainly not an option. Heck, the colors on the screen still blended together in those rainbow lines. She could practically feel the static from where she sat. The entire house was filled with things that would make any antique expert salivate.

Especially the mirror.

The mirror. Her thoughts always turned back to the damn thing. She was getting just as obsessed with it as her grandpa was. It had gotten to the point where some days Camren had to convince him not to spend all his time in front of the thing. He seemed convinced her grandma was talking to him, giving him answers to questions he didn't even know how to ask anymore.

Camren wanted it gone.

It needed to be gone.

She waited until her grandfather fell asleep in his chair, like he did most nights now. Ash had curled up in his lap after he put the bowl of peas aside. Normally Camren would have blanched the peas and cleaned up the mess, but she didn't want to wake her grandfather.

She crept from the living room.

The old house seemed to pop and crack more than usual. The darkness seemed to breathe down her neck, waiting to consume her. Part of her wanted to hide in her room, but she was braver than this, damn it. She took a deep breath.

Her grandfather's room was quiet, eerily silent. Of course, it wasn't like there would have been an echo of the violence that had happened earlier. She approached the antique mirror, not wanting to look at her reflection. Her heart pounded, and she had to wipe sweaty hands on her jeans.

Taking a deep breath, she looked up, her eyes widening.

In her reflection, she was skeleton thin, cheekbones protruding sharply. Half of her face was rotten, with a gaping hole where her eye had been. Her dark hair with the rainbow streaks was stringy and hung in patches at the sides of her head.

She looked dead.

She looked like she had risen from the grave.

Camren let out a cry and clapped a hand over her mouth to muffle the sound. The mirror had to go. And this was probably her only chance. She wretched the damn thing off the wall, nearly collapsing from the weight of it, but she held on tight to the frame. The silver filigree dug into her palms, making them sting.

Seeing her reflection like that, maybe her grandfather wasn't crazy. What if there was something off about the mirror? Granny had died in front of it; maybe that had somehow changed the heirloom. Weren't mirrors usually associated with the supernatural in all the urban legends? What if the hallucinations brought on by Alzheimer's weren't actually hallucinations and Grandpa was really seeing something? It could explain Ash's strange behavior. Animals were said to be attuned to the paranormal.

Camren was a horror movie fanatic and loved her thriller stories and this sounded straight out of one. Of course, she hadn't expected to ever be living in a horror movie. She wasn't about to mess around with something that could be possessed. That was why the mirror had to go.

Stuffing matches into her pocket, she hauled the mirror outside. There was no moon, and she'd forgotten a flashlight. It didn't matter, though. Even in the dark, she knew her way to the burn pit. She passed between the house and the old wooden two-car garage. Something skittered out from the entrance, making her jump, but she clung to the mirror.

The stench from the burning pit was stronger. An old fire still smoldered casting a faint glow in the darkness. That was good; it would make the job easier.

Would a mirror burn? Was it safe? She'd read somewhere that mirrors used to be made of mercury, and the mirror was pretty old. But it was a little too late to think of that now. She set it next to her on the damp ground, face down so she couldn't see any reflections within it. Camren went to work, starting up the fire again. This was something she'd done so many times before. It didn't matter now that her hands shook, and her fingers felt clumsy.

It didn't take long until she had the fire roaring again; bigger and brighter than it had been before. The flames felt warm against her chilled body.

She stooped to pick up the mirror, turning it to get one last look. This time, her reflection was normal, but something was behind her. She shrieked. Her knees buckled, and she fell back away from the pit. The mirror fell on top of her, knocking the breath out of her lungs.

"I told you not to touch it," her grandfather snarled.

Ash perched on his shoulder, something Camren hadn't

seen in the looking glass, a growl coming from deep within the gray tabby's throat. The fresh wounds on her arm stung from the memory. He crouched as if ready to pounce. Her cat, who'd been the sweetest little guy ever, looked at her like he hated her. Like she was a threat.

"Grandpa!" She shifted the mirror off of her, laying it back on the ground. "Grandpa, it has to go!"

He stalked toward her; the menacing rage etched into his face monstrous. The laugh lines were gone, replaced with a furrowed brow. His nostrils flared as he panted like a rabid animal. His features were so twisted, she barely recognized him. Her lips trembled; the tears felt like acid rolling down her cheeks.

"I warned you not to touch her mirror," he snarled.

He had a python-grip on her wrist. She couldn't remember him being this strong in ages, and he had never done anything like this before. He dragged her away from the trash pit. She dug her heels into the ground, but it didn't seem to bother him. If anything, it made him stronger. She felt more like a child now than she had in a long time. She screamed and tried to yank away. Whimpered as she plucked at his fingers, trying to free her now tingling hand.

Ash peered at her from her grandfather's shoulder, giving her a haughty look before jumping down. The message was obvious. She deserved this. Ash trotted ahead of them, leading the way. Camren fought harder when she realized where he was taking her. She didn't want to hurt her grandfather, but she slapped at his arm and yanked as hard as she could. She screamed his name, wailing, though the sobs didn't faze him.

"You will not damage the mirror. It is for my granddaugh-ter," Lawrence spat. He jerked her toward the large dirt mound. She stumbled as his words registered.

"Grandpa. I—I am your granddaughter," she said. Some-how, he held on to her as he yanked open the wooden cellar door. The chain rattled as the door came up and the horrible screeching sound echoed. She fought back a scream. A thick spider crawled across the top step. Probably just one of many. The eerie cold crept up from the depths, like a ghost inviting her in. The old pit was on the brink of collapsing. It had been built with nothing but dirt and wood. They didn't even use it for storage anymore. It was just a hole in the ground. With a door that could be locked from the outside.

"You're the monster that stole her face. And I'll find out how to get her back. You hear me? I'll get my Camren back. The mirror will fix this," her grandfather sneered. Ash let out a meow, an agreement.

Camren spoke, to argue, but Grandpa gave her a tug and a shove. She lost her footing, tumbling into the musky pit. The door to the cellar slammed shut before she even hit the ground. She landed on the cold damp earth and the darkness swallowed her up.

She thought back to the image she'd seen in the mirror of herself as a walking corpse. Maybe the mirror actually was special. Maybe it had shown her a vision of her own grave demise.

THIS ISN'T AN ILLUSION

BY MIRIYA GREER

MERCURY STRUGGLES TO BREATHE AS HE SPRINTS down the neighborhood sidewalk, silently counting the houses as he goes. The counting is supposed to be a distraction, but it's falling short of being helpful. His left arm is scraped and bleeding, along with both his shins, which sting in protest as the cold air rushes against the raw skin, but his injuries are the least of his worries.

Eventually, he comes upon a home painted a soft yellow with a muted red front door. All the curtains are closed, save for one on the first floor, allowing him to just barely glance into the blue-walled living room.

As he makes his way up to the front door, his stomach sinks lower, telling him to turn away now and leave. Nothing good will come from this, he knows. But it's also his duty to deal with the mess. He *caused* it, and now he needs to fix it.

He raises an arm to knock, but the door flies open before he can begin, revealing one *very* angry man dressed in a green oil-stained t-shirt and black pants.

Mercury slowly lowers his arm.

"Hi, Keito..." he says with a sheepish smile, hoping it'll

remedy the already sour mood. But looking into Keito's soulless green eyes, he sees nothing but fiery rage staring back at him.

"What in *Hell*, Mercury!" Keito yells, his shout echoing up and down the quiet street. Mercury flinches. "Why is my sister a *cat*?!" Keito waves a hand down at the floor, and Mercury sees a small golden-furred tabby trot over to stand by the angry adult's side. It stares up at him with bright blue eyes, sitting up on its hind legs and giving Mercury the best frown it can; its eyes narrowing and jaw shifting into a small feline frown. Mercury can't help but think that it's still kind of cute...

"*Well*?" Keito's enraged voice snaps Mercury from his thoughts.

"Well..." Mercury echoes quietly, his aching shoulders rising with his ever-growing anxiousness, "I may have tripped—"

"*Clearly*," Keito hisses back through barred teeth. He opens his mouth to continue but pauses as the cat next to him gently rubs its head against his leg with a small purr. Keito's expression goes from angry, to reluctant, to annoyed within seconds. His gaze drops to the tabby, and a small smile slowly creeps across his lips before turning back to Mercury and folding his arms. His eyes flicker up and down, studying Mercury's injured legs and arms, the cool blood running down his skin. The knees sting painfully in the breeze.

Finally, Keito lets out a reluctant sigh. "Why don't you come in and clean yourself up?"

Mercury can't help but give him a thankful smile. "Thanks."

He steps into the house, Keito shutting the door behind him. The cat leaps towards Mercury and brushes her body up against the uninjured part of his bare leg, making it tingle from her soft fur. He can't help but chuckle, careful not to move or else risk stepping on the poor animal.

"Eva, let him go to the bathroom," Keito tells the tabby. Eva meows and eloquently slips through the doorway to the living room.

"Bathroom's upstairs," Keito tells Mercury as he steps into the living room after the little cat. "The door's open. Bandages should be in the medicine cabinet. I've got to make sure Eva doesn't accidentally tear the couch up. Call if you need any help."

Mercury nods, even though Keito doesn't see it. "Okay."

His legs ache as he climbs the stairs to the second floor, both from running and his earlier fall. His yellow shorts are also somewhat scuffed, but not damaged, and his white tee only has a single smear of dirt on it. Well, a rather *large* smear, but it's nothing that won't wash out with a washboard, some soap, and a little elbow grease.

Mercury steps into the bathroom and glances at himself in the mirror. His blond hair is wild, small clumps of brown dirt still trapped within the strands. His tired golden eyes stare back at him. He plucks a small yellowing leaf from the rat's nest atop his head and drops it into the sink with a heavy sigh. His shabby appearance reminds him of his turn-of-the-16th-century self, which he doesn't mind much. Though he suspects Keito would mind if Mercury wandered around like the serf he once was.

What a nightmare...

When Mercury makes it back to the staircase, his knees and elbow all bandaged up, he finds Eva sitting patiently at the bottom, staring up at him as if she had been waiting there the entire time. Her tail slowly curls behind her into strange shapes. She must really enjoy having a tail.

Keito appears in the living room doorway, leaning against the doorframe, and lets out a small sigh of impatience. "You're done."

Mercury reaches the bottom of the staircase and bends down to come eye-to-eye with the tabby. The cat gives a feline grin and steps up to Mercury's face, touching her nose to his lightly.

"You like being a cat, huh?" He hums, running a hand slowly along Eva's back. The cat purrs softly for a moment, then slowly lies on her side in front of him, clearly enjoying his petting. Her ears droop low and her tail settles into a still half-curve.

"Well, *I'd* like my sister back to normal," Keito says, folding his arms, "if you don't mind."

Mercury's hand pauses, and he shifts onto his knees, expression thin. "I don't know if I can..."

Keito's eyes light up with a dangerous spark, and he stands upright in the living room doorway.

"*What*?" he growls.

"Not if she's like this!" Mercury cries in a panic. "I've never *permanently* turned a human into an animal before!"

"Well, you'd *better* figure something out!" Keito jabs a finger down at Eva. "I'm not letting her stay like *that*!"

Mercury turns back to Eva, her curious eyes staring up at him. Eva's not supposed to be a cat, even though she's very much a cat person at heart. He scratches the underside of her chin, making her purr once more. He smiles back half-heartedly. She's still a very cute cat.

"I'm sorry..." Mercury says. "My foot got caught on a rock and I fell..."

He had only been on the ground for a few seconds when

he had gotten Keito's text. In all caps. Telling him he was in a lot of trouble.

"Well, how about you *stop* falling for once," Keito says. "Remember what happened *last time* you tripped and fell?"

"I blew up the town hall..." Mercury mutters.

"Be glad it happened on a holiday," Keito says. His gaze then strays to his sister, and his brow furrows into slight worry. "Well, what *can* you do to fix her?"

Mercury shakes his head. "Nothing that will bring her back forever."

Keito is silent as Mercury continues to pet Eva. Mercury wishes he could make everything right again; he really does. If only he knew what kind of magic he randomly produced *this* time.

Sadly, there is yet to be an explanation for why he creates a random magical discharge whenever he falls. So far, he's killed grass, created a tornado, froze the mall in the middle of summer and blown-up town hall, none of which is within his skill set. And now he's turned Eva into a cat and doesn't know how!

"So, what you're saying is that this *isn't* an illusion?" Keito asks.

"Not that I can tell, no," Mercury replies.

Keito pinches the bridge of his nose and lets out a long sigh. "I need to think on this for a bit. Are you hungry?"

"A little."

Wordlessly, Keito steps into the dining room, assuming Mercury will follow. Mercury gives Eva one last scratch. With a cat sigh, Eva stands and arches her back, her claws pinpricking at the carpet.

In the dining room, Mercury pauses. The dinner table is covered in a mess of scrap metal, wiring, and an assortment of tools, leaving little room for even a drinking glass.

"Were you making something?" Mercury asks.

"Yeah," Keito replies, staring at the mess. "Though sadly, it isn't a grand project."

"What is it supposed to be?"

"A vending machine of sorts. You've seen one, right?"

Mercury nods. "I have. Can't you just buy them, though?"

Keito lets out a snort and shakes his head sharply. "We've got no use for a regular vending machine. And this thing *will* need my sister when it's done." The inventor shoots Mercury a sideways glance, and Mercury's stomach churns with sickening shame.

"Well," Keito asks, "what do you want to eat, magic boy?"

"PB&J," Mercury replies quickly. It's pretty much the only thing he'll eat for lunch.

"Right. C'mon, Ev. You'll need to show me where everything is." The inventor strides into the kitchen, Eva meowing behind him. Even with one of them stuck as a cat, the twins are as close as ever.

Mercury takes a seat, not bothering to touch the mess of metal on the table next to him. He'll just keep his plate on his lap. He stares into the kitchen, watching Keito place Eva on the kitchen counter. The cat pauses for a moment, staring up at the cupboards above her. Raising a paw, she points at a cabinet, and Keito swings the wooden door open to reveal racks of glass vials, each filled with a different colored substance, capped with corks, and labeled with white masking tape and black sharpie.

Keito holds Eva up to the vial racks. The cat's head flicks left to right, up and down, as she studies the vials. Raising her paw, she motions to three different vials, careful not to touch the racks and possibly knock them all down.

Keito sets the cat down on the tile floor, pulling down the three vials and retrieving plates from a different cupboard.

"I thought permanent transformations were part of your magical skill set," Keito says over his shoulder.

Mercury shakes his head, even though Keito can't see him. "No. I fabricate temporary appearances, kind of like costumes. Illusion magic doesn't turn humans into cats."

"Is there any kind of magic that *does* turn humans into cats?"

Mercury looks down at the floor. "Not that I know of..."

Keito slides a plate in front of Mercury's down-turned face. The white bread sandwich oozes with dark purple jam, creating small purple puddles around the bottom slice. Despite the unusual runniness, the sandwich appears normal, as if made with store bought food. Keito balances a second plate in his other hand.

"Thanks," Mercury says. Keito grabs a seat next to him and pulls out his cell phone, leaving his own sandwich untouched in his lap. Something flashes in his emerald eyes.

"What are you doing?" Mercury asks, the peanut butter thick against the roof of his mouth.

Keito's eyes dart up. "Good news, bad news."

Mercury's stomach drops another couple of feet, and the sandwich threatens to come back up.

He clears his throat the best he can. "W-What?"

"I have someone I can call and ask about... Eva. However, her boyfriend is coming in an hour to pick her up."

"And... what does *that* mean?"

A malicious smirk spreads across Keito's lips. "You think *I'm* angry? *He* is going to lose it. And I'm not letting you leave until you fix my sister. So, I'd recommend fixing her before he gets here."

Eva's fur brushes against Mercury's legs as she weaves her way under his chair. His lips twitch, flickering between a soft smile, and a worried frown.

"Well, make the call, then," Mercury urges.

"Hm, I don't know if he's busy right now or not..." Keito chuckles maniacally.

"*Please*, Keito, it was just an accident!"

"Fine. I'll call," Keito says, tapping away at his phone again. Mercury looks down at his half-eaten sandwich, his appetite completely gone.

"Hi, Hal," Keito says into his cellphone. "How are you doing?"

...

"That doesn't sound very boring."

...

"Well, I'm doing fine, but Eva's a cat right now."

...

"Yes, you heard me. She got turned into a cat."

...

"No, she didn't make a demonic sacrifice. Why would you think she'd do *that*?"

...

"Remember Mercury? He says it was an accident but doesn't know how to reverse it."

...

"Yes, he says it's permanent."

...

"No, I don't think he's versed in the demonic arts at all."

...

"Hang on, I'll ask." Keito lowers the phone and asks Mercury, "Are you a demon?"

Mercury scowls back in offense. "Of course, I'm not!"

"Of course, he isn't!" Keito echoes into his phone, poorly mimicking Mercury's outcry.

...

"Yeah, I know you just wanted to check."

...

"Well, he *is* about five centuries old and still looks about sixteen, so I don't blame you..."

Mercury shoots Keito a glare. He doesn't like to be reminded of his actual age.

Keito rolls his eyes and ignores him. "Uh-huh... Mhm..."

...

"Well, I've got one, but it's at dad's house down the street, and I really don't—"

...

"Well, yes, but—"

...

"You demons—"

...

"No, I've not got an issue with *you*! I just think you guys need to change some of your rules."

...

"Right, you just push papers, don't you?"

...

"You're *my* paper-pushing demon..."

...

"Love you too. Bye." Keito hangs up the call and turns to Mercury. "We need a mirror and some of your magic drawings."

Mercury frowns. "Runes?"

"Yes, those. And I need to run to my dad's house and get a mirror."

"Why?"

Keito presses his fingers to his temples. "Look, I can't keep track of all these different supernatural entities and their superpowers myself. I got you wizards confused with demons. *They* do the permanent transformations."

"Oh." Mercury isn't familiar with the magic demons use, but now Eva's transformation makes a little more sense.

"Eva can show you where the paper and pens are," Keito says, standing from his chair. He sets aside his untouched sandwich. "If I leave now, we should have enough time to get this thing finished before her boyfriend arrives."

"Okay..." Mercury nods slowly. "What kind of runes do I need to draw?"

"I think he said protection, transformation, and human-esque depictions. Do you know any of those?"

"Yes."

"Good." Keito then points down at the floor where his sister lays under Mercury's chair. "Stay out of trouble, Ev. I'll be back soon."

<hr>

The mirror takes up the entirety of Keito's trunk and backseat. It shines in the afternoon sunlight, beaming through the front windshield, making it difficult for him to even glance in its general direction as he drives home.

It also didn't help that no one had cleaned the mirror in an-age-and-a-half, making ancient dust tickle his nose.

Slowly, he pulls into his driveway and makes sure the mirror won't slide and break all by itself before exiting his vehicle. The moment he emerges from the car, he erupts into a short sneezing fit.

"I got it!" he calls as he throws the front door open, his stuffy nose making his voice thick.

"Great!" Mercury calls from the living room. Keito steps into the doorway to see the boy kneeling on the floor, pen in his hand, scraps of paper spread before him. Eva lays next to him, her tail slowly waving. Her bright blue eyes look up at her brother when he appears and she gives him a melodic *meow* of greeting.

He can't help but angrily stare at Mercury for a moment. Some part of him still wants to completely humiliate the boy. But he also wants his sister back. Sooner rather than later.

"I can't lift the thing out of the car myself," Keito says. "I've still got seven more runes to draw."

"Out of how many?"

"Thirty-six."

Keito growls under his breath and walks away. He's not waiting for Mercury to finish his little art project to unload a mirror from his car. He *can* actually do it himself, but it'd be easier for Mercury to use his magic. None of this would be happening if it wasn't for the wizard in the first place.

He trudges upstairs and opens the hall closet. It's full of odds and ends, mostly standard cleaning supplies. Keito reaches in to grab a seemingly inconspicuous short iron rod.

"I'll deal with it, then," he says on his way past the living room, not waiting for a response from Mercury.

He pops the trunk of the car and presses the rod underneath the mirror. The little contraption buzzes and shifts in his hand, spidering out from his fingers and latching onto the sides of the mirror with silver talons. Keito steps back and lets his machinery work its own modern magic.

The spider device wraps the mirror's wooden frame in a thin layer of metal, which then extends over the reflective surface, sealing it away beneath a glossy silver coat. The process takes a minute to complete, but once finished, the antique mirror is now encased in a film of durable steel. With any luck, if he ends up dropping the mirror, it shouldn't break too badly.

He slides the mirror out through the trunk and rushes back to the front door as fast as he can before he loses his grip on the mirror.

Readjusting his grip on the mirror's sides, he quickly ducks it through the doorway, too short for its massive length. And the mirror really is *long*, almost scraping the ceiling of the hallway. It won't fit through any of the other doors, not without another person. And said "other person" is still too involved in his chicken scratch.

"We're doing this in the hallway," he announces.

"Okay," Mercury replies.

With that, Keito taps the metal covering twice, which makes it hum and vibrate once more. The metal coat disappears from the mirror, the metal rod reforming. Keito scoops it up off the ground and slips it into his pocket as Eva scampers out of the living room and bounds towards him. She circles his left leg and rubs up against his shoe with a smile on her feline face and a purr in her throat. Mercury emerges with a small pile of paper a moment later.

"I'm ready," he announces.

"That's good to hear," Keito says. "Let's get this over with."

He takes the mirror and pulls it away from the wall, giving Mercury enough space on the backside to stick up his papers onto the aging wood.

"Okay, they're all up," Mercury says after a moment, sliding out from behind the mirror.

Keito shimmies the mirror back up to the wall and gently sets it into a balanced lean. It sways in his grip, making him worried it'll fall or simply break apart if he were to let it go. Somehow, miraculously, he manages to back away from the mirror and have it stand on its own perfectly. He can't help but let out a sigh of relief.

"It should only be her reflection," Keito informs Mercury, gesturing to the wizard to step back. Together, the two stare at Eva, sitting alone in front of the mirror.

"Nothing's happening," Keito mutters quietly, fearful of making any sort of loud noise.

"Maybe it just needs a moment?" Mercury suggests in an equally quiet voice.

So, they all just stare in silence, Eva's slender tail the only thing moving. Keito doesn't know what he's expecting to happen—Hal didn't have enough time to tell him those details—but he sure is disappointed so far.

Eventually, Eva gets up and inches closer to the mirror. Keito and Mercury both exchange momentary looks of unease and confusion before turning back to the enfolding scene. Eva reaches out to the mirror's surface with a paw in hesitance. The moment the tip of her claw touches the reflective surface, it *ripples*.

Like a stone cast into a pond, waves emanate from her touch across the surface. Eva jumps backwards, ramming herself into the wall behind her with a soft *thump*.

No one moves as the ripples slowly fade back into stillness.

Once again, the brave little tabby inches towards the mirror once again, extending her paw with new confidence. The ripples are much more violent as she strikes the mirror's surface like it's a mouse. She doesn't jump back as before, watching the ripples up close and personal.

And then she plunges through the mirror.

Bloop!

Keito inhales sharply, his body stiff. Should he panic now, or panic in another five seconds? Is this supposed to happen? Will Eva come back out of the mirror, or will he need to dive in to rescue her?

Bloop!

His breath leaves his lungs in a rush as the mirror comes to life once more. Out steps his sister, with reflective silver rolling through the strands of her long blond hair and down the white cotton of her lab coat as she shields her sapphire eyes from the light of the hallway. But most importantly, she's still wearing her cat ear headband, a birthday present he'd given her years ago.

Eva lets out an airy sigh and turns to face Keito and

Mercury, the two boys standing in the hallway as still as statues.

"Kei..." she mutters, stepping towards him on shaky legs. He rushes forward to embrace her just as her knees buckle from her weight, and she leans on her brother heavily for support to keep standing.

"You're okay now," he assures her. "C'mon, let's get you seated on the couch."

The two siblings slowly make their way into the living room, where Keito helps lower Eva onto the couch. She leans back and stares up at the ceiling with an empty gaze, Keito standing over her, his brow furrowed in concern.

"Ah, man," she sighs wistfully, "I'll miss being a cat."

"You will?" Keito asks, his tone airing on the side of mild amusement.

"Having a tail was cool," Eva says, holding up a finger and attempting to wave it back and forth, poorly mimicking a cat's tail. "And the back scratches were nice, too."

"I need you so I can finish my machine," Keito responds with an exaggerated eye roll. "Plus, you've got a date tonight."

Eva nods in agreement. "That's fair."

Mercury steps in, holding the papers he put on the back of the mirror once more, his gaze downcast.

"I'm sorry I turned you into a cat, Eva..." he mutters.

Eva smiles. "These things happen, don't they?"

Still, Mercury's shameful expression deepens, and his gaze darts to the doorway, probably wondering when and how he'll make his escape.

"Everything's fixed now," Keito assures him, awkwardly patting Mercury's shoulder. "You can go home if you want."

Mercury nods. "I'm sorry I caused you two this much trouble. I hope the rest of the afternoon goes well for you both. And, uh... say hi to your boyfriend for me."

With that, the boy quickly hurries out of the room.

"Don't fall!" Keito calls after him as the front door opens and shuts once again.

"What's the likelihood he's going to trip on his way home?" Eva jokes half-heartedly.

"Too likely," Keito grumbles back.

MARLA

BY RICK POWELL

IT WAS THE PURRING THAT WOKE ME IN THE MIDDLE of the night. The lace gossamer curtains greeting my eyes waved delicately, as if to get my attention. Through the partially opened window a full moon beamed. The night spring air wafted my way, cooling my sweated brow, as I felt Marla tread on my shoulder—no doubt to get to the windowsill above my head—to sit there as she usually does; sometimes napping long into the morning.

Granny always said her orange tabby slept over her head to keep the bad dreams from invading her sleep. But bad dreams are the least of my worries. I wished Marla could help get rid of my current dilemma.

It has been two weeks since Granny's funeral, and I still cannot believe she's gone. When Granny was here, she would find a way to soothe me when I was sick, either with her home-made chicken soup (the recipe she took to the grave) or with hugs and kisses that surpassed all medicines. Every time I saw her, she made me feel like a little girl and not a thirty-two-year-old woman in the stages of a crumbling marriage.

I could not tell if my body ached from needing her now, or from the flu or whatever bug had hit me these last few days.

The purring above my head continued. A slow, melodious sound that seemed to shudder the yellowed, cracked wall; a murmur that traveled up to the darkened, cobwebbed ceiling above my head.

I groaned. *There is so much to do to fix this house.*

Two weeks and I haven't started on what I must do to clean, to hire the repair people, and all the other minutiae.

I craned my head to look up at Marla. The huge cat turned her head down at me. I could faintly see her green eyes look down, almost judgingly.

"In the morning," I said through a rasping voice while knowing, technically, it was morning. "I will start in the morning."

I coughed and turned to the side, pulling my knees up to my chest. Hopefully, I'd feel better by then.

I listened to the purring as I drifted back to sleep.

"When are you coming home?" Dale demanded. The handset of the wall phone perched precariously on my shoulder as my chin held it in place. I tried to keep my hand steady as I poured another cup of coffee. My eyes squinted as the morning sun glared through the flowered curtains of the kitchen window. I could imagine Dale's reddened face on the other end of the line.

"I told you a few days ago, I don't know." Turning from the window, I tried to get his image out of my head. The phone cord pulled taut as I walked to the center of the kitchen, the cradle attached to the wall shifting with the strain. "I am calling her lawyer today about the will—"

"You haven't called him yet!" Dale shouted, cutting me off.

I gritted my teeth. A crackle sounded through the handset. "There is a lot to do here. I have been busy." My voice was raspy. *Jesus, I need more coffee to deal with him now.*

"Busy... sure." The coldness in his voice gave me a chill.

I put the carafe on the plate of the coffee maker as gently as possible. "I just need a little more time. Once things get rolling with the lawyer, I can decide what I can do with the house—"

"There is nothing to decide. I thought you were going to sell it. It's a crumbling money pit full of old junk. She was living on public aid and cat food, for Christ's sake! We could have had all of this taken care of by phone instead of flying you over a thousand miles away to get stuck there. Speaking of phone calls, why don't you answer your cell? This landline connection is horrible."

"Dale, *please.* I just need a little more time." I couldn't bear looking at my cell with his photo on the home screen.

"Time? For what? We discussed this. I could have had everything settled in a few days. I had connections fifteen minutes from her house that could have gotten it done in a snap. What's the hold up?" I wince as I hear the thud of the palm of his hand smacking the Rosewood desk that he loved.

"This isn't just *her* house. I grew up here. It was *our* house. You know she took care of me when my father skipped out. And then again when mom died when I was sixteen. Granny did so much for me. I... I... owe it to her to... to... take care of things..." *Fuck, I am letting him get to me. Hold it together, Valerie. Stand your ground, as Granny always told you.*

"Well, you aren't taking care of shit. Purposely, like you always do. I swear you do this just to piss me off. You are the worst when it comes to the most critical of thinking skills. Where would you be if I wasn't around to take care of the day-to-day stuff? I swear your head is in the fuckin' clouds!"

"Dale..." My body trembled, and I couldn't utter another word.

"I gotta get to a meeting. Just call me when you have a better excuse."

The click of the disconnection was more of a relief than anything. It matched our marriage.

"Well. That didn't go well," I whispered as I hung up the phone.

I heard a tinkle behind me as Marla jumped up on the kitchen counter; a slight meow emanating from her as she sat down and stared up at me with a twitching tail.

"You heard that, huh?"

Meowing again, she lifted her paw towards me.

I picked her up with a grunt, cradling her enormous bulk in my arms. I scratched her ear as I rub my face into the nape of her neck, trying not to think about Dale's late nights at work. The so-called "board" meetings. How did seven years of marriage come to this?

I turned Marla's face to mine. "I just need more time, right? Gotta figure out what I need to do. About a lot of things. But first, we need to feed you, and find something for me to eat."

Sighing, I opened the refrigerator, greeted by the mostly bare shelves except for the partially opened can of cat food haphazardly covered with Saran Wrap. The half-eaten bagel from the convenience store from the day before sits next to it, like a loyal friend.

"Well, girl. It looks like this afternoon I gotta go shopping for some groceries."

Time for me to take care of some shit.

First on my list, after talking to the lawyer, was finding the papers he'd requested. I started with Granny's dresser, chock-full not of clothes, but random things she'd collected over the years. My hands paused, and I let out a gasp when I felt the smooth surface of a mirror.

I saw the edge in the bottom drawer—the personal papers and the will tied neatly with a faded blue ribbon covering most of the mirror. A rush of memories filled my head.

The mirror was a French antique brass vanity mirror that swiveled through its center—the stand of which has been long gone. It seemed to not have been touched in years. The foot long, oval-shaped mirror had tinges of corrosion around its molded rococo decoration that suggested that it was generations old.

I gently put it on the dusty top of the dresser and turned it upward to look into it. Seeing my reflection—haggard eyes and a lined mouth belonging to an older woman than one in her early thirties—I traced my fingers around the gilded oval frame, refusing to look into it again.

"Granny, how long have you had this?"

Time seemed to shift, and I was sitting on Granny's bed, watching her put away clothes and staring in the mirror in its proper place on the wall.

"Oh child, longer than I remember," Grandma said. "The mirror was my Granny's, and she left it to me. It goes back generations."

"It looks broke."

"No, sweetie. It used to have a base to sit on the tabletop but that is long gone. Missing during the war. That's why I hang it in my room."

"War? Which war?" I'd had no idea my granny was involved in anything like that.

Granny chuckled. "Don't fret yourself. It was a long, long

time ago. My Granny Marla had many amazing tales of her youth."

"Marla? Like your kitty! Your kitty is named Marla!"

"Oh yes. My Granny Marla took care of me like I take care of you."

"I love your kitty. She sleeps with me at night. She curls up near my head, and she touches her paw to my face." I giggled.

"And Marla loves you. Just like I love you, honey."

"Can I take this mirror to my bedroom? I will take good care of it!"

"Maybe when you are older, honey. I promise to give it to you."

"Promise?"

"Promise."

"I love you, Granny."

I didn't realize I was crying until a tear hit the aged glass, running down the glass like my reflection itself wept. With a deep breath, I pushed away the memory to focus on the duties at hand. About to place the mirror back into the drawer, I hesitated. Would it get forgotten about if I put it away? The days ahead would be full of disposing and donating what I could, and I did not want this to be lost.

With the papers clutched in one hand and the mirror held close to my chest, I proceeded to the kitchen, my stomach leading the way and reminding me of the lunch I hadn't had yet.

Tossing the papers next to a vase of dried, wilted flowers on the kitchen table, I opened the refrigerator to finish the remnants of the bagel, but my tired eyes widened in surprise.

I didn't remember the antique Tupperware bowl from before, but maybe I'd missed it; it sat on one of the empty shelves below my line of vision and was filled with a liquid. Granny had always stored her special chicken noodle soup, the cure for everything from heartache and sorrow to the common cold, in this container.

As I pulled it out, the aroma of vegetables and refreshing broth seemed to seep from it. A questioning grin filled my face —the first in many days—as I cracked the lid and saw the hefty chunks of chicken, celery, carrots, and the like.

How did I miss this before? I wondered. With the condition I was in, this was just what I needed. How many other things had slipped my notice these last few weeks?

With my stomach growling in anticipation, I retrieved a pot and heated it up on the gas stove. Stirring the soup, I realized today was going to be a better day, no matter what lay ahead.

Bringing my gigantic bowl of soup to the table, I propped the mirror up against the vase, petting Marla with one hand while I consumed the heavy broth, the chicken perfectly seasoned, the carrots soft and the celery crunchy.

The cat purred as she lay there next to the vase, her eyes closed in contentment.

***

"Your grandmother was a wonderful woman," the cherub-faced lawyer said as he sat behind the ornate oak desk. The afternoon sun shining through the blinds of the window to the right of me accented his reddened cheeks as he gave a sincere grin. "I have known her for years. She was a very organized, meticulous, and gentle woman. I wish I had more clients like her."

Leaning back in his leather chair, he motioned to the paperwork in front of him. "She had everything more in order than even I did, if I don't say so myself."

I sighed with relief. "That is good to hear. I have been...

having a lot going on these last few weeks and was concerned that things would just drag out."

"You do not have a thing to worry about. She had no outstanding debts. Heck, she came in every first of the month to pay on the life insurance policy she had. Even kept her checks made out to the utility companies in advance in case she... she passed away."

"I am relieved she had a policy."

"Nothing extravagant, mind you, but a good sum for whatever you may need in times like these. Since the house and property are in your name now and all."

I looked down into my folded hands in my lap, clutching the wrinkled Kleenex. "I don't know what to do yet. This is all so much to take in now."

"Well, I am here to help with anything you need. Just call me day or night. My brother-in-law has a real estate office at the edge of town. He deals in this sort of thing all the time. He can help you if you want to sell."

"I appreciate this. More than you know." I coughed into the tissue.

Looking at me with a sympathetic expression, he cleared his throat. "Is there anyone here to help you? It is a massive undertaking, I understand, and you seem under the weather."

I avoided his gaze. "I haven't been feeling well, and she left everything to me. No other immediate family. I was all she had." I sniffled, shifting in the chair. "My... husband is caught up in work and is still up north. This will pass. Just sinuses or a head cold."

He sat back—his eyes somber. "I totally understand. A little chicken soup does wonders."

I replied with a slight grin. "I had some earlier. It has helped."

He placed his large palms on the table, looking at the papers before him. "Listen, let me go through a few things here to make this as easy a process as possible, and I will call you tomorrow to finalize everything. Just go home and get some rest."

I rose out of the chair, taking his outstretched hand to shake. "Thank you. For everything. I have to run some errands first. Groceries and such, y'know."

"Of course. Talk to you soon."

As I walked out of the office, I felt my phone vibrating in my purse. Ignoring it, I got into my car and drove out of the parking lot into the late afternoon sun.

Dusk was approaching when I finally parked Granny's old Buick in front of the sun-faded garage door. I'd tossed the idea around with moving some of the stuff inside the garage to make room for the car—a thought I quickly banished after seeing the multitude of cobwebbed cardboard boxes of holiday decorations, collected knickknacks and such—but looking at the full grocery bags in the back seat, I wished I had. Getting the overly full bags would be easier going into the house from the attached garage than it would be trudging them up the cracked, uneven walkway from the driveway to the front door.

Granny had become very acquainted with the cashier at the grocery store; a cheerful, obese woman by the name of Harriet. Harriet recognized me as when I'd stepped into her line and was sympathetic as she said how much my Granny meant to her. More than one tear formed in her eyes, and she inquired about Marla, talked about the times Granny and Harriet talked, and other niceties (a conversation not appreciated by the other customers waiting behind me in a line that was growing by the second) as I nodded uncomfortably and thanked her many times.

I realized when she heartily waved goodbye and bellowed

out to give "that old precious kitty a hug for me" that the cat seemed old even when I was a young child. I had no knowledge of any cat living longer than twenty years or so.

Sitting in the car now, I thought about Marla. What would I do with her? Dale abhorred any sort of pet, and there was no way she could go to a shelter or with someone she didn't know. Was Marla ever seen by a vet? I have never known Granny to bring the massive feline anywhere for medical purposes. Maybe there was some paperwork somewhere I needed to find.

My growling stomach pushed aside my concerns about my grandmother's cat as I concentrated on gathering up the groceries and carrying them inside with as few trips as possible.

Marla watched me nonchalantly from the kitchen table, her bulk taking up a good portion of the table. The mirror leaning on the vase of flowers reflected her hindquarters. I sat the last bag down, my attention drawn to the vase.

A few of the stalks seemed a little greener than a few hours ago. There was even a new bud full of color on the dead flowers full of color. How odd. The opaque liquid filling the vase was in no way providing any sort of nutrients or acceptable means of hydration. I should've thrown the flowers out, but they were low on my priority list.

Pouring the milky water out of the vase to replace it with fresh, I heard the buzz of my phone from my purse. After fixing the flowers, I retrieved my cell and looked at the screen.

Dale had called many times, leaving a voicemail each time. I knew what messages consisted of and didn't bother to listen to them.

Tossing the cell back into my purse, I picked up the handset off the phone on the wall and punched in Dale's number, my index finger hesitant on the last digit.

"About time!" Dale growled at the other end.

"Sorry. I was running errands. I had to meet with the lawyer and—"

"You could've called me from the cell. Why do you keep using this damned landline phone?"

"Bad call service." A lie anyone could see through. I was too irritated and hungry to think of anything creative.

"Did you meet with the lawyer yet? Did she leave you any money?" he asked, a quick change in tone.

I sat at the kitchen table, my shoulders slumping. *Wow. After not returning any of your calls, you could have at least asked if I was ok.*

"He said that he would call me tomorrow. He's still finalizing paperwork, but it looks like she left me something. Not much, but it'll help me get things in order and such."

"Just crunching the numbers to up his fee, I bet. You should've let me call—"

"Dale, I gotta go. I have had a long day. I have a headache and am hungry."

"You're not going anywhere. We need to talk about—"

I hung up. After staring at the phone in mild shock for a few moments—mostly at myself for being so assertive—I took it off the hook, and placed it on the counter, just in case he tried to call back.

As an afterthought, I went into my purse and turned off my cell. Tossing it onto the table, I caught my reflection in the mirror. My eyes reminded me of Granny's, and then I was back in the past again.

"Gran, quit fussing so. I am nervous enough." I'd said, applying the mascara to my lashes.

"I just don't like that man, dear. He has shifty eyes."

"You never like anyone I dated. He is nice to me. He has a promising future."

"Yes. He told me. Many times. He'd better stay nice to you. His flashy car and flashy style just don't sit right with me."

Granny looked over my shoulder into my reflection in her mirror. "You're putting on too much makeup. You look like a harlot. Does he like it that way?"

I turned my head away to glare at her. "Granny!" I exclaimed. "What a thing to say!"

She stood back and straightened her posture. "Humph! I guess that is a yes."

I'd straightened, turning my body this way and that to check for any wrinkles in my summer dress. "He will be here any minute," I said, avoiding the subject. "I'll be late. Don't wait up."

"There will be a plate of dinner for you in the fridge when you get home," she muttered as she walked out, arms crossed.

"Dinner," I say to my reflection in the mirror propped against the vase. My eyes look like mine again, tired and beaten. "If only I'd listened to you then, Granny. Though score one for me for standing up to him today." I unpacked the groceries, smiling to myself as I pulled out a small pack of steaks. "Well, Marla. We are going to eat good tonight. What do you say? Candlelit dinner for two?"

The orange tabby meowed approvingly.

I awoke the next morning feeling refreshed. Stretching with a yawn, I spotted Marla perched in her usual spot on the windowsill above my head. I craned my head with a smile, squinting my eyes to the soft glow of the sun as it filled my room.

"Morning, sunshine." I said to Marla as she turned her head towards me; eyes still closed as her long tail gave a gentle twitch in answer.

I cannot believe how well I slept, I thought. *We should have steak more often. Well, if our house and all the repair work don't drain me dry first.*

I stilled, realizing what I just thought.

Our house.

I cannot get rid of it. This house has so many memories of good and bad times. How in the world will I ever convince Dale, I can keep it?

I pushed myself up to a sitting position. A combination of the chicken soup, the steak, and the spring air—a much needed change from the condo I shared with Dale within the smog-laden city limits—must have done wonders to whatever was ailing me.

As I got out of bed and went to the kitchen, draping myself in one of Grannie's silk robes, I detected a faint flowery scent. The fragrance seemed to envelope me as I approached the kitchen table, Marla close at my heels.

I gasped.

Washed aglow in the beams of the morning sun was the vase. The water inside seemed to shimmer, matching the array of colors from the blossoming flowers. Not a decayed stalk, nor a wilted leaf, was present.

Marla jumped up to the vase, rubbing her jaw on the mirror, knocking it slightly askew with her actions.

"What in the world?" I asked in one exhaled breath. "This should be impossible!"

I gently touched one of the petals; the warmth from the sunlight seeming to transfer to me. I sniffed the flowers, the sweet, flowery fragrance flowing around me.

"Well, it looks like I am not the only one feeling better. Amazing what some fresh water and sunlight can do."

It was going to be a good day. A day full of promise.

After preparing a hefty breakfast—eggs, bacon, and toast for myself, and one of Grannie's china saucers filled with canned cat food for Marla—I spied the handset of the phone still off the cradle from the night before. I should have felt guilty for cutting off all communication ties with not just Dale, but the outside world in general, but considering the rest I'd gained, I felt more than justified.

With a sigh, I placed the handset back on the cradle and retrieved my purse to turn on my cell phone. I tossed it back into my purse with a slight sense of revulsion and dreaded any calls that I would receive today (aside from the lawyer). Considering how forward I was with Dale yesterday, I had a feeling of confidence that I had not felt in a long time. I decided I would not let him, or anyone else, ruin my day.

I was making a list of things to accomplish today while waiting for any news from the lawyer when I heard the familiar vibrate from my phone in my purse. Grudgingly retrieving it, I was already prepared for a verbal battle, when I glimpsed the number. Not recognizing it in the slightest, I was leery when I tapped to answer.

"Hello?" I asked cautiously.

"Hello. Is this the wife of Dale Nerverough?" a firm, male voice inquired.

"Yes. This is she."

"I'm sorry, ma'am. We have been trying to contact you all night. This is Officer Hawkins from the Seattle PD. There's been an accident with your husband last night."

"Oh, my god! I... I had the phone off! What happened? Is he—"

"There was a car accident. He is at Harborview Medical. What is your location? I think you need to get there as soon as you can. Are you nearby?"

"What? No... no. I am at my house... my grandmother's house in Massachusetts... is he ok?"

I felt the phone in my hand vibrate for another incoming call. Ignoring it, I slumped down into the dining table chair.

"Ma'am, you need to get to the hospital as soon as you can."

"I can't! I'm too far away. I'll have to get a flight..."

"It's best if you get here as soon as possible, ma'am."

The phone vibrated again. It was an associate of Dale's.

"I have to go. Others are calling... shit..."

"Ma'am—"

I ended the call, tossing the phone on the table. It sat there vibrating, slightly rotating, as if it was some upturned, frightened insect, eager to get my attention.

I put my hand to my mouth in shock. Trembling, I stared at the phone, knowing I should pick it up, but could not summon the will to do so. The shock I felt was not concern for what happened to my husband and the unknown condition he was in but from my hesitation to know anything further.

It was not fear that his condition would be worse than I could imagine but the inconvenience of leaving the house.

It wasn't that I couldn't leave, it was that I wouldn't.

I lost track of time sitting there at the kitchen table, staring at my reflection in the mirror I held in my hand, my face slowly turning to a shadow in the encroaching dimness that enveloped the kitchen, the remnants of the morning's breakfast still untouched. Dusk was creeping along the kitchen window above the sink when I glanced at the phone still lying in the same position as before, a rectangular shadow on the yellowed linen covering the table.

I knew deep in my heart Dale did not survive the accident.

I was still trying to grasp the emotion that was wavering

through me like waves in a disturbed river. An emotion I had not felt in as long as I could remember.

Relief.

I knew part of me should feel guilty for having such an emotion at a time like this, but try as I may, I didn't feel it.

I wanted the relief to last as for long as it could, fearful I'd never experience it again. I knew I had to attempt to pick up that phone, make the calls needed, get a flight, and so much more, but I wanted to hold out just a little while longer.

Marla gently rubbed her ear on the edge of the frame; her purring a pleasant substitution for the silent vibration of the phone.

I knew I would get through whatever the future has in store, and I had a feeling my future was here. At our house in Salem. I knew I would survive, and I would not be alone.

As if in confirmation, in the dusk that filled the kitchen, I discerned a translucent hint of a hand extending out of the polished glass to pet the brow of Marla lovingly.

Granny will be waiting.

About the Authors

Anthologies are wonderful places for new and established authors to get their stories into the hands of others. We wouldn't have this anthology without the creativity and imagination of our authors, so we wanted to take some space in this book to celebrate each of our wonderful writers. So, in the order of their stories, here's some information about each of them.

Dennis K. Crosby

Dennis K. Crosby grew up in Oak Park, IL and completed his undergraduate work at the University of Illinois-Chicago. With a degree in Criminal Justice, he spent six years working as a Private Investigator. His love of learning about, and better understanding people, led him to pursue a master's degree in Forensic Psychology. During his studies, Dennis transitioned to social service, and since 2008, has worked primarily with men and women experiencing challenges with mental health and addiction. He continues to be a staunch advocate of mental health reform, social justice, and efforts to combat homelessness.

Dennis always had a passion for writing but did not pursue the finer points of the craft until later in life. After leaving Illinois and moving to San Diego, Dennis connected with the local writing community where he strengthened his talents and understanding of the art of writing and the business of publishing. To further supplement his writing skills, in 2018, Dennis completed an MFA program at National University.

Now, he is the award-winning author of the Amazon bestselling urban fantasy novel, Death's Legacy, released November 2020, and its follow up Death's Debt, released November 2021. The bourbon loving Chicago Cubs fan and deep-dish pizza connoisseur is continuing his work on his Kassidy Simmons series and writing weird and creepy short stories in his spare time. A self-proclaimed geek and lover of pop culture, Dennis still lives and writes in San Diego, CA.

EVAN BAUGHFMAN

Much of Evan Baughfman's writing success has been as a playwright, his original plays finding homes in theaters worldwide. A number of his scripts are published through Heuer Publishing, YouthPLAYS, Next Stage Press, and Drama Notebook. Evan has also found success writing horror fiction, his work found recently in anthologies by Improbable Press, 4 Horsemen Publications, and Grinning Skull Press. Evan's short story collection, *The Emaciated Man and Other Terrifying Tales from Poe Middle School*, is published through Thurston Howl Publications. His novella, *Vanishing of the 7th Grade*, is available through D&T Publishing. More info is available at amazon.com/author/evanbaughfman

Lara Yamada

Lara is an aspiring young adult fiction novelist. She's published five short stories across two anthologies. She lives in Columbus, OH with her husband and daughter. She absolutely loves swimming and living overseas and plans to make her way to Germany for a few years. She looks forward to her writing time every day and blends common relationships with a hint of fantasy and paranormal. She spent six years Active Duty in the U.S. Navy and currently enjoys stay-at-home parent life with a toddler to focus on fitness and writing.

Kari Shuey

Kari Shuey & Angela Perry

Supermom by day, romantic suspense author by night, Kari strives tirelessly to ensure no hero escapes his emotions and no heroine lacks her happy ever after. On the opposite side of the genre spectrum, Angela sublimates her repressed fury from her job in corporate America into torturing her fantasy characters. One fateful October day, they meet in an online writing group, and the unexpected happens: they become fast friends and writing partners. Was it chance? Kismet? A curse from an

Angela Perry

ancient crone in Stockholm, Sweden? Read Mathias and decide for yourself.

Kari Shuey grew up in Utah and currently lives in Idaho. Writing romance and suspense novels is a deep-rooted passion that she only started sharing recently. She loves trying new things and diving into crazy projects.

Angela Perry lives in Utah and actually enjoys her career as a software business analyst. Reading and writing consume most of her free time, but she also likes rockhounding, hunting down dead people, and staring at the stars.

Kari and Angela adore their partnership but appreciate their friendship even more. They are obsessed over their latest project and hope you love Mathias as much as they do.

A.E. SANTANA

A.E. Santana (she/her) is a Southern California native who grew up in a farming community surrounded by the Sonoran Desert. A lover of horror and fantasy, her works can be found in *Latinx Screams*, *Demonic Carnival III*, and other horror anthologies. She is the managing editor for Kelp Journal & Books; the moderator for the horror book club, The Thing in the Labyrinth; and the communications manager for Full Circle Players, a theatre company in Riverside, California. She is also a founding playwright for the East Valley Repertory Theatre in Indio, California. She was the former editor for *The Coachella Review*'s monthly column on diversity in literature, Voice to Books. A.E. Santana is a member of the Horror Writers Association, Denver Horror Collective, and has participated in several horror panels, including "No Longer the Scream Queen: Women's Roles in Horror." She received her MFA in fiction from the University of California, Riverside's low-residency program. She graduated from California State University, San Bernardino, with a bachelor's degree in mass communications and a minor in script writing. Her associate degree in journalism is from Imperial Valley College. Her perfect day consists of a cup of black tea and her cat, Flynn Kermit.

S. FAXON

S. Faxon is a creative warrior. On top of writing dark fantasy, horror, urban fantasy, and thriller novels, Sarah is a cover designer, and loves teaching high schoolers English Language Arts. She is a member of the Horror Writers Association, the Independent Book Publishers Association, and San Diego Writers, Ink. Sarah is the co-founder No Bad Books Press, LLC. with her business partner, Theresa Halvorsen.

S. Faxon's books include: *Blood Lords, The Animal Court, Foreign & Domestic Affairs, Tiny Dreadfuls,* and *Origins: The Blue Dragon Society.* Sarah has also co-written two books with her business partner, Theresa Halvorsen: *Lost Aboard* and *How to Be A Successful Author and Not Lose Your Mind.* To see her complete works, visit Sarah's <u>Goodreads</u> and sign up to receive insights from her weekly <u>newsletter</u>.

DONNA MARIE WEST

Donna Marie West is an educator, translator, author, and freelance editor. She has published some 500 drabbles, short stories, and non-fiction articles in a wide variety of Canadian and American magazines, web sites, and anthologies. She loves the unusual and unexplained, and often finds ways to weave these themes into her stories.

She has published three books to date. In 2019, she co-authored a collection of horror-themed short stories and poems entitled *HAUNTED HORROR*, which is currently out of print as the publisher closed its doors. Her first novel, *NEXT IN LINE*, was published in September 2020 by an independent American publisher. It is also out of print for the moment as that publisher has also closed. Her second novel, *THE MUD MAN*, was published in April 2022 and is available at the usual places.

Donna spends her precious free time reading, writing, and doing research for her current projects. She lives in Québec, Canada, with her long-time partner and two beloved kitties. You can follow her on her Amazon author page or her public Facebook page, both under her name.

CHRIS BANNOR

Chris Bannor is a speculative fiction writer who lives in Southern California. Chris learned her love of genre stories from her mother at an early age and has never veered far from that path. Her stories have been published in over two dozen anthologies and range from horror and science fiction, to fantasy, romance, and steampunk.

When not writing, Chris enjoys spending time with her family and binge-watching sci-fi and fantasy shows. You can chat with Chris on Facebook @chrisbannorauthor. To keep up to date with her musings and new releases, visit www.ChrisBannor.com

DONNA KEELEY

Donna Keeley has been writing for years but is only recently getting her works to print. A long-time science fiction and fantasy fan, along with historical novels and mysteries, Donna enjoys crafting stories that are complete in a single volume. Her paranormal mystery Series features real, haunted locations and uses the documented ghosts as part of the fictional mystery story.

Her home in San Diego County provided her with the inspiration for her first volume in the series, *Having a Whaley of a Time*, which takes place at the historical Whaley House in Old Town San Diego, which appeals to lovers of mystery, ghost stories, and cats. Upcoming locations for stories include the Queen Mary in Long Beach, California, the Alamo in San Antonio, Texas, and Loretta Lynn's haunted plantation in Hurricane Mills, Tennessee.

Donna's first published short story, "Reflections of Hawthorne," appears in *The Mirror* anthology published by No Bad Books Press, LLC and she looks forward to future collaborations.

K. R. CERVANTEZ

K. R. Cervantez is the author of *Mischief's Game*. She's happily married with an amazing family. She has a young self-proclaimed spider expert for a daughter and an adorable dog named Karma. Born and raised in Texas, she now has the opportunity to travel to many places. She creates her own worlds through stories so that others can enjoy them as well. Though she dabbles in a few different genres, her favorites are young adult, paranormal and thriller. When she's not writing, she is enjoying a good book or watching some of her favorite shows. She's wonderfully nerdy in all the best ways. She likes anime, mangas, and comic books. Coffee, chocolate, and pickles are a way of life for her, just not always at the same time. She is passionate about her collections of blankets, snow globes, and journals that are too pretty to write in.

MIRIYA GREER

Miriya Greer has been teaching herself how to write creative young adult fiction since middle school, and always pushes her peers to dream their very best. She has experimented with many forms of storytelling, such as in animations and student films. Beyond writing, Miriya is a third culture kid who enjoys gaming in her spare time and sometimes indulges in manga and anime.

This Isn't an Illusion is Miriya's way of introducing the reader to her two largest creative endeavors with one short story. *Shadowbound* and *(Not Your Average) Robotics Class* have both been developed over the course of her high school years and continue to grow as she begins her adult life. Her plans are to get these stories published, alongside her many other ideas she has yet to begin writing as well. Ambitious and bright, her creativity knows no bounds, with the stars being her only limit.

RICK POWELL

Rick Powell lives in Oak Forest, Illinois. He is a lover of horror and dark fiction and his poetry and

stories have appeared in numerous publications including Infernal Ink Magazine, and most recently, *Lustcraftian Horrors: Erotic stories inspired by H.P. Lovecraft*. His poetry books consist of the titles *My Soul Stained My Seed Sour* and *More Regrets Than Glories*. His collection of short stories is titled A Vault of Whispers and he has a novella titled *Teacher*.